Rx Missing

Decorah Security Series, Book #10
A Paranormal Romantic Suspense Novel

By Rebecca York

Ruth Glick writing as Rebecca York

Published by Light Street Press
Copyright © 2015 by Ruth Glick
Cover design by Earthly Charms

ISBN: 978-0-9906321-5-3.

PROLOGUE

From his F18 fighter jet, Lieutenant Commander Mack Bradley looked down on a scene of destruction.

His chest tightened as he listened to the choppy, breathless voice of a man trapped in his disabled Humvee.

"This is Whiskey Two Romeo. Convoy hit by roadside bomb. Rockets. Automatic weapons. Repeat Whiskey Two Romeo. The bastards are in the hills to our left ... Sweet Jesus ... can you lay down fire ... ?"

Mack kept his own emotions in check as he came around to the convoy's position.

Stay cool. Do your job. Then get the hell out.

When he got the all clear, he executed the attack, diving on the enemy, delivering a series of 500 pounders before zooming upward again. A typical Middle Eastern bombing run, he thought with satisfaction as he headed back toward the carrier.

Only this time, a heat-seeking missile zeroed in on his engine. He felt the teeth-rattling impact, saw the fire warning light and knew he had only two choices. Go down with the plane or eject.

No choice at all, really, because the escape procedures had been drilled into him.

Adrenaline surged through his system, as he began sending out his call sign and location. There was no time for fear or worry. He simply acted automatically.

1

"Mayday, Mayday, Mayday. This is Lightning 22 ejecting twenty miles south of Senadar. Repeat this is Lightning 22."

No response came in the moments he had left in the crippled aircraft. He had to trust that they'd heard him as he pulled the handle on the seat between his legs, got his body into position, and prayed that the chute would open.

Seconds later, the seat blasted out of the cockpit with a force of 17 Gs.

As he tumbled through space, there was nothing more to do but wonder if he was going to live or die.

Then, like the old clichéd phrase, his entire life flashed through his mind. He smiled as he tasted his mom's chocolate chip cookies. Felt again the joy and pride of catching the winning touchdown in the Allegheny County championship game. The scenes came fast and furious, each with the emotions of the moments he'd spent on earth. Hunting expeditions with his dad and twin brother. Midshipman at Annapolis. Flight training. The wild bachelor party before his disastrous marriage.

The sum total of his life. He'd thought he had years to enjoy it, but it had turned out to be so damn short.

He tried to grab on to a good memory—like back when he and Grant had always known what the other was thinking. Instead he had a few stabbing moments to remember how he and Gail had hurt each other. Then everything went black.

CHAPTER ONE

At one in the morning, the Winston Funeral Home was quiet as a tomb. The back door had been locked, but Grant Bradley had learned long ago how to get in and out of the right and wrong places.

After slipping his lock picks back into his knapsack, he quietly closed the door and stood for a moment in the dimly lit hallway, listening for signs that he'd been discovered.

But no one dead or alive challenged him. If a rent-a-cop appeared, he could always say that grief made men do strange things.

He'd seen that as a CIA agent. Experienced it for himself when he'd abandoned a promising career as a spook to come home and stare into space until Frank Decorah had asked him to join Decorah Security. That hadn't worked out so well either. Not when he'd compared his talents to the other guys in the agency. They had several werewolves on staff and a guy who picked up memories from objects he touched. Grant had felt like a second-class member of the team. So he'd left after a couple of years—over Frank's objections. Frank had said Grant's talents were going to blossom, but he'd seen no evidence of it. And when Dad had gotten too old to handle his Western Maryland outfitter business, Grant had come home to take it over.

He'd asked Mack to join him. The Bradley twins working as a team again, but his five-minutes-older sibling was still flying high as a Navy pilot, and look where it had gotten him.

3

Mack was in one of the reception rooms. His body was supposed to be pretty beaten up, which was why the casket lid had been screwed down tight.

But that wasn't going to stop Grant from saying good-bye—his way.

He'd coped with the grief of his and Mack's friends all day, plus the awkward encounter with his brother's ex-wife.

Now he was alone. Very alone. As kids, he and Mack had gotten inside each other's minds. That talent had faded when they'd matured. But not his love for his brother.

A man with a mission, he moved stealthily toward the coffin which sat on a velvet-draped table. He wasn't going to break down. He was just going to pay his final respects to a man he had loved with an unwavering steadiness, even when they'd had their disagreements.

As he rested his hand on the polished mahogany of the coffin top, he spoke quiet words to his brother—his best friend.

"I've missed you, Mackie. Sorry you didn't get home for Christmas this year. And that we didn't get a chance to do some fishing in the fall." He dragged in a breath and went on, struggling to hold his voice steady.

"Remember the fun times we had together? On the football team. At Ocean City after our senior year. And remember that fight with the Frostburg guys in back of the bowling alley where we got busted by the cops, and Dad had to bail us out. He was mad as hell, and we had to chop wood for the entire winter to make up for that one."

He knew he was stalling because he didn't want to look inside the coffin. Yet he *had to*. Was that a little bit of the old psychic ability coming back to him? He scoffed at the rationalization and kept talking.

"I brought you some stuff that you might like to have. That championship football that you kept in your room. Your high school ring. And a Snickers bar. Your favorite."

Grant rummaged in the knapsack again for a Phillips screwdriver, then went to work on the screws that held the lid down.

He carefully set them on the velvet-topped table before closing his eyes for a moment and saying a prayer for strength.

Steeling himself, he lifted the lid with a jerk and looked down into the coffin. A gasp escaped his lips as he struggled to understand the horror of what he was seeing.

Mack's body was not in the coffin.

Not Mack or anybody else.

Nestled in the silk padding was a featureless man-sized prosthetic *thing* in place of his brother's remains. Like a department store dummy, only it must have been a lot heavier, since it had to make up the mass of a physically fit, full-grown man.

Emotions smashed through Grant in quick succession like interior shotgun blasts as he struggled to come to grips with the implications.

Shock. Then relief. Then a hundred questions. Was his brother alive—and somewhere else? And if so, where?

That was followed by worry and fear. If he was alive, what had happened to him?

In the end, Grant was left with stone-cold fury as he pulled out his cell phone and took a picture of the lifeless hulk that mocked him in the coffin. Hardly able to keep his hand steady, he mailed the picture to his computer, then to cloud storage.

What the hell was going on here, and where was his brother?

If Mack wasn't at the Winston Funeral Home, where the hell was he? And why?

He lowered the lid of the coffin but didn't bother screwing it down, then closed his eyes, feeling like a fool yet desperate enough to try the old trick he and his twin had shared.

"Mack," he whispered. "Can you hear me Mack?" He kept projecting the message, but there was no answer, and finally he gave up.

Well, gave up on the attempt at mental contact—but not on finding out why his brother's supposedly mangled body had been replaced by a faceless dummy.

CHAPTER TWO

The moment Mack Bradley woke, he knew something was very wrong. At first it was just a kind of free-floating anxiety. A dread he couldn't identify. But it soon solidified into a more concrete apprehension that sent a shudder skittering over his skin.

Lying very still, he stared at the open wooden-railed canopy above the wide, soft bed. Cautiously he sat up for a better view of the room and saw a writing desk in some English antique style he couldn't name and a hallway leading to a marble bathroom. Across from the bed was a long, inlaid dresser with a flat-screen TV.

He threw back the covers, swung his legs out of the bed, and noted that he was wearing a navy blue warm-up suit with a white tee shirt under the jacket.

Feeling a little unsteady on his feet, he kept one hand on the bed as he dug his toes into the thick Oriental carpet.

He was in what looked like a very expensive five-star hotel room, not that he'd spent a lot of time in luxury digs.

But he could be on leave. Maybe Dubai or Bangkok? He'd enjoyed R and R in both those locations and splurged on deluxe accommodations. This was the kind of room he'd expect there.

Had he gotten drunk out of his mind last night? And ended up here alone?

Possibly, except that he didn't remember checking into any hotels. Or dressing in the warm-up suit.

The memory gap made his chest tighten painfully. Wracking his brain, he tried to dredge up the last thing he remembered. From somewhere in the stratosphere, it zinged back to him with gut-churning force.

He'd just dropped a couple of five hundred pounders on some murderous insurgents when a missile had come whistling up his ass.

Now he was here.

Or was the mission all a nightmare?

No. He remembered dropping the bombs. Remembered the crippled plane. All that was real. Not like this place.

His stomach clenched. Where was he *exactly?*

Heaven? Hell? A hospital?

Was he dead or alive?

Or what?

He balled his hands into fists, digging his nails into his palms, struggling to ground himself.

He had vague memories of another bed. Narrow. With high sides. A woman taking care of him, speaking to him in a soothing voice, telling him he was safe now. That everything was going to be okay.

He'd opened his eyes and looked at her. Struggled to answer her, but he hadn't been able to get any words out. Now the scene skittered out of reach. Had *that* just been a dream?

No. Like the bombing raid, it felt real.

"Calm down," he muttered aloud partly to hear the sound of his own voice. "You'll figure this out."

He flexed his arms and legs, feeling the muscles work, reassured by the physical sensations. Pulling up his tee shirt, he looked down at his abdomen and chest. No injuries as far as he could tell.

Which was good. Right?

In the bathroom, he switched on the light and saw a huge soaking tub, a separate glassed-in shower, a black granite vanity with double bowls and a separate little room for the toilet.

A razor, shaving cream, deodorant, toothbrush and toothpaste were neatly lined up on the shelf above the sink.

The toothpaste tube was new. So he'd just gotten here, right? Which was why he didn't remember this place.

But shit, he must have checked in. And he didn't recall that at all.

He stared at himself in the mirror. Dark hair. Dark eyes. The scar on his chin from when he'd fallen out of a tree when he was eight. He'd been dazed, and Grant had helped him back to the house.

Relief washed over him that he recognized the man who stared back.

But where the hell was he?

His heart began to pound as hard as it had been pounding when he'd pulled the ejection lever on his seat and blasted out into the naked sky. What if ISIS had scooped him up after he'd bailed out?

And then what? They sure as hell wouldn't have installed him in this palace. Instead he'd be in a dark, dank cell with cockroaches for companions. Not a luxury hotel. Unless they were trying something very tricky? Like that TV series where they convert the guy to Islam.

He was about to fill the glass from the tap to moisten his dry mouth when he saw a bottle of water on the sink. Maybe he'd better use that.

After taking a drink, he said his name aloud.

"Mack Bradley. Lieutenant Commander, US Navy. Born and raised in Cumberland, Maryland. Cumberland High School. Naval Academy. Divorced."

That last part hurt. He'd been in the Gulf when Ginny had written him to say she couldn't take the long absences anymore, and she was moving on with her life, with a guy she'd met at work, it turned out.

He rubbed his hand against his chin. No beard stubble. But he didn't remember shaving.

Repressing a curse, he walked into the dressing area and looked at the neatly hanging clothes, everything from jeans and tee shirts to more dressy sports clothes. Curious about the size, he took down a pair of well-washed jeans. They fit comfortably, and he folded the sweatpants onto the hanger before pulling on a black tee shirt, then a pair of running shoes and socks that were also his size.

Once he was dressed, he looked toward the wall of drapes in the bedroom. When he thought about pulling them aside and taking a look at his surroundings, his stomach clenched into a tight, hot knot. "Jesus. What do you think?" he muttered to himself since he was the only person here. "That you're going to see smoking pools of brimstone?"

Or maybe a psychiatrist on the balcony who would explain that he was in a high class mental hospital, and he wasn't getting out any time soon.

Teeth clenched, he pulled the heavy fabric aside and peered out onto a lush green lawn bordered by beds of tropical foliage. Magenta bougainvillea climbed up a high stucco wall bordering a forest. From his vantage point, it seemed that he was on the second floor of a two-story building. Perpendicular to his room, he saw another wing of the hotel.

The peaceful scene was reassuring, until he noticed that nothing was moving out there. Not a person. Not a bird. Not an insect.

When he snatched up the phone on the bedside table, he heard no dial tone. But there had to be someone at the desk downstairs. Someone who could tell him where he was. Except that he was going to feel like an idiot getting into that kind of conversation. Perhaps it was better to play it cool, scout around, and see what he could find out.

Before exiting the bedroom, he looked toward the television set. There was a remote lying under it, and he picked it up and pressed the power button. He got a menu with movies, games, TV. There was a large selection of all three, but he found no live television—only prerecorded shows. If he was bored, he could watch some of this stuff, but he wanted reality, not canned programing.

He turned off the set again and walked down a short hall into a living room furnished in the same opulent style as the bedroom. His keycard was in a slot by the door.

The plastic rectangle had a red and gold design of scrollwork and arches that looked vaguely Middle Eastern—or Indian—but there was no hotel name.

After pocketing the card, he stepped into the hall. No brimstone. Only a long runner of Oriental carpet over polished wood at the sides of the hall, and striped paper on the walls.

He was in room 222.

After noting the number, he hurried to a wide marble staircase which led to a lobby furnished with groups of comfortable couches and chairs.

All very tasteful and very expensive. A stage set with no people.

And when he tried to turn on a computer on the check-in desk, nothing happened.

He thought about cupping his hand around his mouth and calling out, "Anybody here?" Or maybe, "where the hell is everybody?"

But that could be dangerous.

Christ, what if terrorists had taken over the hotel? They'd killed everybody in sight, and they were waiting for the next victim to show up.

But if they'd done it, the attack had been totally silent. Besides, he saw no bodies. No blood. No signs of a struggle like overturned chairs and tables or broken knickknacks on the floor.

He was heading across the lobby when a muffled scream made him stop and reverse directions..

CHAPTER THREE

Following scuffling sounds, Mack came to another wide hallway where a man and woman grappled in a ferocious struggle. He had her back to the wall, and she was trying to extricate herself from his grasp.

The woman was slender, with short-cropped dark hair. She was dressed in jeans and a pretty emerald-colored blouse. Mack was sure he had seen her before, but didn't have time to ponder where or when, because it looked like her attacker was bent on killing her.

Dressed in sweatpants and jacket like the ones Mack had been wearing when he woke up, the guy was tall, blond and at least six inches taller than the woman. He was making harsh, guttural sounds as he tried to wrap his hands around her neck.

"Get the hell off her," Mack shouted as he sprinted toward the struggling pair.

The guy's head jerked around, his steel-blue eyes wide and crazed, as Mack leaped forward, catching the attacker with a blow to the face that made him waver on his feet.

When the woman dodged to the side, gasping for breath, the guy switched his attention to Mack, throwing punches like some mechanical maniac. Or a man with the desperation of insanity.

Mack ducked under the blows, pressing his face into the guy's chest so that the large fists landed on his back.

He slammed the top of his head upward into a bony chin, just as the woman darted in and aimed a kick that caught the attacker in the shin.

He went down from the double whammy, and Mack was on top of him, landing a couple of clock-cleaning punches, surprised that he hadn't even broken a sweat from the exertion.

He waited to make sure the man was out before turning to the woman.

Pale and shaken, she stared at him with round, frightened hazel eyes.

"Are you all right?" Mack asked.

She flexed her arms and legs. "I think so."

"Any reason he should be trying to kill you?"

She shook her head helplessly. "I can't think of any. Did you get hurt?"

"No," he answered, studying her, trying to recall where he'd seen her before. "Do I know you?"

"No."

But she'd hesitated for a fraction of a second, making him wonder if she was as uncertain as he—or lying.

He kept staring at her, cataloguing her narrow face, her slightly shaggy haircut, her slim build. When he tried to place her, he couldn't come up with anything specific, only vague feelings of familiarity.

And protectiveness.

When he saw she was wavering on her feet, he pulled her into his arms, feeling her trembling in reaction to the attack as he cradled her in his embrace.

"You're okay. Everything's going to be okay," he said, wondering if he was speaking the truth as he stroked his hands up and down her back, feeling a shiver travel over her skin. He still didn't know where the hell they were or why.

He liked the feel of her body against his and wanted to keep holding her. To reassure her? Or himself? Or was he simply feeling the need for human contact? In this strange, empty place, he'd finally met two more people, and one of them was obviously dangerous.

"We've got to secure this guy before he wakes up."

Reluctantly easing away from her, he looked back the way he'd come, saw a telephone sitting on one of the desks. When he picked up the receiver, there was no dial tone, like with the one in his room. After yanking out the phone cord, he carried it back to the man on the floor and began tying his hands behind his back. He'd have to get more cord for the legs.

Just in time, because the guy made a gurgling sound and started to stir.

After hoisting the limp form over his shoulder, he carried him to the nearest doorway, aware that the woman was following. Beyond the door was a small office with a computer sitting on a desk, a printer and a brocade sofa, where Mack laid the captive.

He moaned, still dazed. When he focused on Mack, anger flared in his eyes, and he jerked forward.

Mack pushed him back onto the couch. "Take it easy."

"Not fucking likely," he bellowed, his face turning red with anger as he struggled against his bonds.

"You speak English?"

"Of course I do, you moron."

"How did you get here?" Mack asked.

"Jesus! I don't know. I was on my motorcycle. Then ... I don't know." He stopped and looked around as though the surroundings would tell him something. "I woke up, and here I was. Get your paws off of me, you son of a bitch."

"Calm down." He glanced at the woman. "Did you just get here, too?"

"Yes."

Taking his eyes off the guy for a moment was a mistake. Even though he was tied, the captive lunged at Mack who jerked back, barely avoiding a savage bite as large white teeth clanked together.

14

The woman gasped, and Mack spared her another quick look as she stood with a horrified expression on her face.

The bound man glared at her. "Stop pretending it's not your fault."

"It's not!"

He answered with a snort.

"There's something wrong with him," she whispered.

"Apparently." Turning back to the man, Mack asked, "Can you tell us your name?"

"Jay Douglas. Want to make something of it?"

"Great to meet you," Mack answered.

"And who the hell are you?"

"Mack Bradley."

"That doesn't mean jack shit to me." He jerked his head toward the woman. "What's your name, bitch?"

"Lily Wardman."

He snorted. "You're lying."

"Why would I?"

"So I can't hex you."

"Right." Mack sighed. "Sorry, buddy, if there are other people here, we don't want them untying you and getting hurt."

"Fuck you."

The guy turned his head away, but the brunette kept her eyes on Mack as he rummaged in a desk drawer and found some packing tape, which he first used to secure the guy's ankles, then as a gag, working from the back so he wouldn't get bitten. When he saw the guy trying to pull the phone cord off his wrists, he reinforced the bindings with more packing tape, inwardly cringing at what he was doing. Yet it was obviously necessary to keep the man from hurting someone.

Lily stared at the captive. "He needs medical attention."

"Uh huh. We'll call the house physician—as soon as we find where the staff went. Meanwhile, all we can do is keep him immobilized," Mack answered as he wrote a note on a sheet of printer paper. "The guy in here attacked unprovoked. Keep your distance. Do not untie him."

After signing his name, he backed away.

The brunette stood staring at the man on the couch, her expression uncertain.

"Do you know where we are?" he asked.

Did she hesitate for a split second before saying, "No"?

He'd been thinking he had to get out of here. Contact the authorities. But deep in his gut he had the sneaking suspicion that would turn out to be impossible.

When she followed him out of the office, he closed the door behind them and taped the note at eye level where nobody could miss it.

"I hate to leave him like that," she said, still sounding doubtful. "I mean he must be having some kind of mental problem."

"Right. But he's a danger to himself and others."

"Yes." She agreed reluctantly.

He turned to face her, wondering if he could find anything out by giving more information. "I woke up a little while ago in a bedroom upstairs—room 222. What room are you in?"

"250," she answered automatically, then looked like she wished she'd kept the information to herself. "I came down here to find out what I could."

"Yeah. Me too. What's the last thing you remember? Mack asked, trying to keep his voice as normal as possible. "I mean before you ended up in this insane asylum?"

"Is it an asylum?"

"What do you think it is?"

"It's pretty upscale."

"Yeah. It must cost thousands a month. What about your last memories?" Mack prodded.

He saw a thoughtful look cross her face. "I guess ... driving to work."

"Which is where?"

"Union Memorial Hospital in Baltimore. I'm a nurse on the surgery floor."

"And you never got there?"

"I don't think so." She swallowed and looked down as though she were trying to hide her expression or work out what she was going to say next. "What about you? Are you from Baltimore, too?"

"Western Maryland, but last I remember, I was in an F18 over ... the Middle East," he said, heeding the admonition not to reveal his exact assignment. "I got hit and bailed out."

She dragged in a sharp breath. "Hit?"

"Heat-seeking missile."

"You're lucky to be alive. How ... how did you get here from there?"

"No idea." No use saying he wondered if he *was* alive. Or if this was an outpost of the Twilight Zone.

She tipped her head to the side, studying him. "But you don't remember anything after the plane?"

"Maybe I remember a hospital bed. Maybe I remember *you*." He made that last part a challenge as he kept his gaze fixed on her.

Her breath caught, and some of the color drained from her face. "That's impossible."

"What if you were hurt, too? What if we were in the same hospital before we got here?"

She shrugged, then looked like she was making an effort to stay calm. "I'm not sure of anything." He watched her take in a breath and let it out. "Sorry. I'm ... scared. I mean, I wake up in a strange bedroom, come downstairs, and some guy tries to choke me to death."

"Yeah." He wouldn't go so far as to say he was scared. Not yet. But he was definitely worried about this whole setup.

She made a quick change of subject. "Do you think there are other people here?"

17

CHAPTER FOUR

"Yes." The answer came from Mack's left. He and Lily both turned to see a man and a woman walking toward them. The guy was wearing a running suit. The woman had on a long flowing dress with a bright pattern. She was slightly overweight and looked like she dyed her curly hair dark brown because there was a tinge of gray around the edges. The shapeless dress did nothing to enhance her dumpy figure. But her eyes were keenly speculative, and she looked like she was functioning pretty well mentally.

The guy, not so much. He appeared to be in his late thirties, fit and tanned with close-cropped brown hair and large brown eyes. He kept sticking his hands into his pockets and pulling them out again.

"I need my phone," he said when he caught Mack watching him. "My wife's going to be worried."

"Where were you before you got here?" Lily asked.

"Playing touch football with friends."

"Wouldn't you put your phone down before playing football?"

"Yeah. I guess."

Mack went on to the classic question. "I don't suppose either of you happens to know where we are?"

The woman raised her chin. "I'm betting this is the Mirador Hotel in Agra, India. Five stars and pricey."

Lily looked surprised—and impressed. "What makes you think so?"

"I'm a travel agent. I've been here on a familiarization trip. The place is top-of-the-line as far as luxury goes. With two staff members to every five guests. Male staffers in tunics and turbans. Women in silk saris. Too bad none of them seem to be around to give us any information."

"Yeah," Mack agreed.

"I'm Paula Rendell."

"And George Roper," the man added, his attention barely focused on Mack and Lily as he kept looking around nervously.

"You know each other?" Mack asked.

With an effort, the guy brought his attention back to them and shook his head. "No, but we decided that it's a good idea to use the buddy system."

"Right," Mack agreed.

He and Lily introduced themselves.

"After the initial panic, some of us settled down in the bar. Why don't you join us," Roper said.

"Initial panic?" Lily asked.

"Yeah," Roper said obviously struggling to keep his voice calm. "Like how did we get here? What's wrong with this place? Why aren't the phones working—or the computers? Where is the staff?"

Mack looked toward the double glass lobby doors, thinking he should get the hell out of here instead of standing around quizzing people who didn't know any more than he did.

If he was in India as the Rendell woman suggested, he should call the U.S. Embassy. Let them know that Lieutenant Commander Mack Bradley wasn't dead. But he was willing to bet a month's pay that walking out of this place wasn't going to be so easy.

"I've had enough of this. I'm splitting," Roper said as he started toward the door.

"I wouldn't advise it," Paula answered.

19

"Why?" Mack asked, curious to hear why she sounded so sure of herself.

"Because this is India. Or maybe it isn't." She ran a hand through her bouncy curls.

"The point is, there's an enormous difference between the atmosphere in a luxury hotel in this part of the world and what's on the street. If you've been to India, you know what I mean. Beggars who won't take a polite "no" for an answer. Cows wandering all over the place. People sleeping on the side of the road. Like the movie Slumdog Millionaire, only you're in the middle of it. Take my word for it. You don't want to go stumbling around on your own. There are too many bad things that can happen."

Did she believe what she was saying or was the warning a ploy to keep them where they were. Was she really a travel agent? Or was she here to ride herd on a group of strangers who were struggling to figure out what was going on? Or was someone else the ringer? Another hotel guest he hadn't met yet. Or one he had.

"I've never been out of the U.S. You think this is really India?" Lily asked. She seemed too worried to be in on the joke—if there was one. Or maybe she was a good actress. Like in that Truman movie, where Jim Carrey is raised from birth in an artificial environment, and everybody else is an actor. Even his wife and parents.

The travel agent shrugged. "Is this really India?" she repeated. "Either that or an elaborate stage set."

Which was something like what Mack had been thinking. But what was it *for?* And how had they gotten here?

"We might as well hook up with the other people in the bar," Lily said.

Mack considered his options. He still wanted to get the hell out of here, but he'd come to the conclusion that it would be smarter to get some more information first.

"The bar's around the corner and down the colonnade." Paula pointed toward another exit from the lobby. "I don't know about you two, but I could use some fortification."

She led the way across the lobby and out onto a covered walkway that bordered a courtyard, surrounded by the hotel on three sides. The far end was open, leading to a wide lawn that ended in the high stucco wall Mack had seen from his bedroom window. Beyond that were the trees he'd also seen.

"Are we out in the country?" he asked.

"No. The Mirador's in the city, but most posh hotels in India have a wall and a strip of forest separating them from the *hoi polloi*. A luxury hotel here is its own little world. With security guards at the gate." The travel agent stopped talking and surveyed the scene. "It doesn't feel right."

"What do you mean?" Lily asked.

"The temperature out here seems to be the same as inside. It should be a lot hotter outside the air conditioning."

"So you think we're not really outside?" Mack questioned.

She shrugged, then looked at the blue sky overhead. "No pigeons."

"Pigeons?" Mack asked.

"There are a lot of them in India. They'd be all over that fountain, unless there was a guy standing around flapping a towel to scare them away."

A sudden flash of movement had them all looking toward the trees. A huge black bird came swooping down, circled the woods and disappeared into the greenery.

"More like a buzzard than a pigeon," Mack muttered, thinking it was the first animated thing he'd seen besides these few people.

Paula shuddered and started walking fast—past a brass statue of the Hindu elephant god, Ganesh, to a cluster of cast-iron tables and chairs. Beyond them was a door that led to a softly lighted bar decorated with peacock motifs. It was furnished with comfortable sofas and chairs grouped around small glass-topped tables.

21

Again, no hotel staffer was on duty. But a dark-skinned man with shaved head and young woman with shoulder-length chestnut hair and light eyes were sitting at one of the tables. An athletic looking guy was pacing nervously back and forth. The woman wore the kind of running suit Mack had woken up in. The guy at the table with her wore khakis and a light blue golf shirt.

The pacing guy looked at them. "I'm supposed to be at a lesson in twenty minutes," he muttered. "They're going to fire me."

"They'll understand," Lily said in a reassuring voice.

He stopped and glared at her. "I don't need your uninformed opinion. I need to get out of here."

"Did you try?" Mack asked.

"Oh yeah. The front gate has bars. And on the other side, a couple of tigers were staring in at me like I was lunch."

"Tigers!" the woman at the table breathed.

"Yeah. Like in a zoo. Only I got the weird feeling we're the ones inside."

Mack took that in. Was the guy hallucinating? Making it up?

The man snatched up a glass from the table next to where the other two were sitting and took a swig of what looked like Scotch.

"That doing anything for you?" the dark skinned guy asked.

"Hell if I know."

"But you can taste it?"

"Taste it? Yeah I can taste it."

The seated black man picked up the glass in front of him and sipped. "This is supposed to be gin and tonic, but it might as well be distilled water for all I can tell."

Lily's head snapped toward him. "You're sure?"

He thrust out the glass. "See for yourself."

When she took a small sip and said, "Gin and tonic," he glared at her. "Someone else try it."

The travel agent picked up the glass and sipped. "Gin and tonic."

"Christ," the black guy exclaimed. "Then what the hell's wrong with me?"

Mack could feel the tension building in the room, and he could imagine some kind of mass panic attack. "We need to stay calm and figure this out."

George Roper glared at him. "Figure it out how, smart-ass? You have some inside information?"

"I wish I did," Mack admitted. "We could start by exchanging particulars and see if we have anything in common."

"What particulars?" Roper demanded.

Mack took a seat at a table adjacent to the others. "Name, occupation, where we were before we got here."

"What does it matter where we were?" Roper demanded.

"Because those are our last memories before we got here," Mack answered.

Lily sat with Mack. Paula and Roper sat together. The ones who had already met Mack and Lily repeated what they'd said earlier.

"I'm in insurance," Roper added.

"You look more like a football player," the woman at the table said.

"Used to be. In college. I play for fun now."

"And you live where?" Lily asked. "Boston."

"I was on a train from DC to New York," Paula told them.

Mack looked at the pacing man who was too restless to take a seat.

"Chris Morgan. Ski instruction. "The last thing I remember is a rundown an advanced slope—to check it out for one of my students."

The black man who'd complained about the drinks spoke up. "I'm Ben Todd. Lawyer. I was at a home improvement warehouse in Alexandria, Virginia. I needed some stuff for a project."

23

"What project?" Paula Rendell asked.

"Is that relevant?" He shrugged, then said, "I'm adding a patio in the backyard."

The woman with the chestnut hair had scrunched down in her seat, obviously hoping to avoid talking.

"And you?" Mack asked.

She gave him a nervous glance. "Jenny Seville. Schoolteacher." Her voice was barely above a whisper, and she looked like she wanted to disappear through the floor. Mack understood the feeling, but he pressed her a little.

"What city?"

"Catonsville, Maryland."

"School was in session?"

"No. We were about to start."

A sudden noise at the door caught everyone's attention.

Another man strode in. He was lean and tanned and handsome, with sun-streaked hair. Wearing jeans, boots and a black tee shirt, he looked surer of himself than anyone else in this damn place. So was he in on the secret joke? Or was he just better at hiding his fears than the rest of the group?

In answer to the inquisitive looks, he opened his hands in a disarming gesture and smiled. "I saw some of you heading out the door and followed."

Mack was instantly on the alert. He didn't like the way this guy had materialized after the rest of them had gathered together. Had he been hiding out and waiting to make an entrance? Or had he finally decided he wasn't going to learn anymore on his own. But why?

"So who are you?" Chris Morgan, the ski instructor, asked from behind the bar where he'd pulled out a bottle of rum and a can of coke. He and the newcomer were the only ones standing.

"Tom Wright. If you want a great deal on a new or used car, I'm your guy."

Well, he did look like the type. Slick and ready to capitalize on any weakness.

"From where?" Mack asked.

"Philadelphia. And you all?"

In turn, the people in the room repeated the personal information.

When they finished, Wright recited back all the names and occupations. Either he had some super ability to memorize, or he already knew who everyone was.

Earlier Mack had wondered about Paula. Now he was thinking Wright could be the ringmaster. Or maybe they were acting together, working the group. Or what about Jenny Seville. She was obviously worried about something. Or was that just an act?

CHAPTER FIVE

Mack clenched his fist under the table, ordering himself to stop making up conspiracy scenarios about everybody here. But he couldn't shake the conviction that *someone* here had more information than everyone else.

You didn't just plop down a bunch of people in a strange environment without keeping some kind of check on them.

Was there a way to trip up the person who knew what was going on? Make him or her reveal the purpose of this place? Or maybe they were all imposters—working a con on Mack Bradley.

He repressed a snort. It sounded insane—and pretty paranoid. Or maybe self-important was another way to look at it. But what *was* normal here?

Partly as a way to get his mind off himself, he made a list of the players—adding observations.

The crazy guy he and Lily had met was Jay Douglas. That was all they knew about him because he'd been too hostile to do more than cuss them out.

She was a nurse from Baltimore. Worried

Paula Rendell. Travel agent. Train to New York. Self-assured but nervous about the buzzard she'd seen flapping over the garden before disappearing into the woods.

George Roper. Insurance. Boston. Hot to get out of here.

Jenny Seville. Teacher. Catonsville. Hiding something.

Chris Morgan. Ski Instructor. Colorado. Angry and upset.

Ben Todd. Lawyer. Alexandria. No sense of taste—which had started in this place?

Tom Wright. Car salesman. Philadelphia. Sure of himself or pretending to be.

Mack Bradley. Fighter pilot. Cumberland and the Middle East.

Nine strangers in the "Hotel California". Why were they here, and could any of them check out?

He kept mulling over what he knew. More of them were from the East Coast, if that meant anything. More of them were men.

"If this is India, how did we get here?" Wright, the car salesman, demanded. "And why India, for God's sake? I never wanted to go there. Never even thought about it. Too dirty. Too many people. And cows wandering around, pooping all over the place,"

There were murmurs of agreement. Apparently only Paula Rendell had considered India as a prime vacation location.

"There are no cows in here," Lily said.

"So far," Roper answered.

Mack studied their faces. While they'd been sitting here, most of the men had gotten a grip on themselves and were putting on what he'd call a brave face.

Lily was also taking in the reactions, the way he was.

Chris Morgan, the ski instructor, looked at Jenny Seville. "You didn't tell us what you were doing before you got here."

"I'd rather not say."

"Everyone else did," George Roper pressed.

"We can skip it," Mack said.

"Why should we?" Ben Todd, the guy with the taste buds missing in action asked. "We're trying to get information."

Jenny looked like she wanted to cry. "It's personal."

Mack raised his voice. "Leave her alone."

"It could be relevant," Todd insisted.

"It's not," she shot back.

Before the argument could go on, Wright, the car salesman, took up the narrative. "If we're saying what we remember last, I was walking my dog and got caught in a thunderstorm."

The statement, and what the others had said, gave Mack something more to think about. Nobody had been home eating dinner, sleeping or reading in bed.

Had they all left their lives around the same time? Or had some of them been in cold storage?

Cold storage? That was a nice way to put it. What if they were all dead? And then what? He could have died when he ejected. But then how had he gotten *here.*

Could they all be on some kind of drug that was creating this illusion? Or what about mass hypnosis?

An old movie he'd seen flashed into his mind. No Exit, about three not very nice people trapped forever in a hotel room in hell.

Jesus! The outlandish possibilities were coming hard and fast. But maybe there were ways to get more information. If everybody was willing to give honest answers to questions.

"What season of the year are we all remembering?" Mack asked.

"Spring," Ben Todd answered.

"Summer," Jenny Seville said, maybe in an attempt to cooperate.

Before anyone else could answer, thunder boomed and a bolt of lightning struck so near the building that the glasses on the tables rattled.

CHAPTER SIX

Grant Bradley picked up the phone and dialed the local home improvement store. As he listened to the various extension options, he heard a click on the line.

Like the clicks every time he used the phone in the past few days. Someone was listening in to his calls. The government? Foreign terrorists who were holding his brother captive?

He snorted. He might have called himself paranoid if he hadn't opened that coffin the night before Mack was scheduled to be buried in the family plot.

He'd charged over to undertaker, Neal Winston's, house and started pounding on the door like a madman.

As the guy had stood blinking under the porch light, Grant started shouting, "Where the hell is my brother?"

Winston stared at him in consternation, obviously reluctant to offend a client. "Your brother? He's in our best parlor."

"Maybe that's what you think, but there's a dummy in the coffin."

The mortician struggled to gather his wits. "Grant, take it easy. I know you're upset, but ..."

"Get dressed. Right now. You've got some explaining to do." He hauled Winston across town to the funeral parlor, slammed the lid open, and pushed the mortician's face into the empty box.

"Where the hell is my brother?" he repeated.

The man's mouth gaped open as he stared at the dummy that was supposed to be Mack Bradley. From the way he looked, it was pretty clear he was just as surprised as Grant.

"Tell me what you know," Grant grated.

"I ... I got the notification from the Navy, the way I always do when it's a case of a guy dying in action. They sent your brother's body from Bagram to Dover Air Base, the way they always do. They asked that the casket remain sealed. They didn't want me to do any cosmetic work on him."

"Is that usual?"

"In cases where the body was badly damaged ... yes."

"Let me see the paperwork."

"Now?"

"Yes. Now."

Winston took him to the office, scrabbled through a file cabinet and pulled out a folder with official-looking documents.

Grant scanned them, the words swimming in front of his eyes. It looked like an official form, but something obviously wasn't kosher.

"Cancel the funeral," he growled.

"We can't. It's scheduled for tomorrow morning."

"Listen, you lamebrain, what do you think—that you're going to put that *thing* in the ground and pretend it's my brother? Cancel the fucking funeral! "

"What am I supposed to tell people?"

Grant thought about that. Maybe his brother wasn't in the coffin, but suppose he was alive and it was dangerous for him if people knew what was going on?

"Tell people there's been a mistake and Mack isn't here."

"Where is he? What am I going to tell everybody?"

"That you realized there was a mistake in the paperwork."

"Okay," Winston agreed, sounding like he would agree to anything so long as Grant Bradley didn't strangle him.

Grant turned and stomped out of the building before he started throwing small objects around the office.

He didn't even try to go to bed. Instead he sat in the living room of his large log cabin, nursing Scotch, straight up. It would have been better if he could have slept because all he could do was speculate with no more information. He began making phone calls as soon as any government offices were open. The conversations proved to be just as unsatisfactory as the one with Neal Winston.

Nobody at the Department of the Navy or the Pentagon knew anything. Or if they did, they weren't saying.

After a week of being shuffled from one bureaucrat or secretary to another, he was angry and frustrated. Unable to concentrate on anything but his quest for information, he cancelled all the wilderness expeditions on his schedule. Family emergency, he'd told his disappointed clients.

Really, he'd known he couldn't give anybody his best until he found out what the hell had happened to his brother—and why someone was hiding the truth.

When he hadn't been able to get any information over the phone, he'd made trips to the Pentagon, Capitol Hill, and even Norfolk, where Mack had been stationed before he'd shipped out. All of the digging yielded no results. As far as anybody knew, it was a bizarre mistake. But how? And why?

Grant had just dropped the receiver into the cradle when the phone rang again, and he snatched it up.

When he answered, a clipped male voice said, "Mr. Bradley."

"Yes."

"This is Colonel Jack Wilson. I understand you've been inquiring about your brother, Lieutenant Commander Mack Bradley."

He dragged in a breath and let it out. Finally, somebody was calling him back.

"Yes, sir. I was notified that he was killed when his fighter jet was hit by a missile. But his coffin was empty."

"I'm sorry. The Defense Department is as distressed as you are."

"I doubt it."

"I do have some information."

Grant felt a spurt of hope which was immediately dashed. Why should this guy know any more than anyone else?

"But I don't want to discuss it over the phone."

"Why not?"

"It's a matter of national security."

"How?"

"I think it would be better if we talk in person."

"All right."

"I'd like to meet at the Franklin Roosevelt Memorial in Washington, DC."

Grant blinked. "Isn't that kind of a strange place?"

"It's a public venue, where we can have some privacy— and be sure nobody is listening in."

He didn't like it, but he said, "All right. When?"

"This evening, around eight."

"I'm four hours from the city."

"But you should be able to make it."

"That's closing time, right?"

"Correct."

He wanted to say the situation sounded ... unorthodox. But he was talking to a U.S. military officer, who was finally going to spill the big secret about his brother. Or was he?

"I'll have to leave right now."

"Thanks for your understanding."

The line clicked off and he hung up. The phone call, the whole setup gave him a bad feeling. But if he didn't keep the meeting, he might never know what had happened to Mack.

When the hotel stopped shaking from the nearby lightning strike, Mack jumped up. "I'm going to have a look outside. Why don't you come with me?" he said to Lily.

She stood. "Yes. The buddy system."

"Me too, man," Roper, the insurance guy, echoed.

Mack worked to contain his annoyance. He'd seen an opportunity to be alone with Lily, and now Roper was horning in. On the other hand, the muscular guy looked like he'd be useful if they were attacked.

By whom? Or what?

That still remained to be seen.

"Okay. Everybody else, stay put."

The car salesman, Tom Wright, tipped his head to one side as he stared at Mack. "Who made you the captain of the team?"

"Better if we don't all put ourselves at risk," Mack answered as he hurried toward the door. Lily and Roper followed.

"What risk?" Wright called after them.

"I wish I knew," he answered over his shoulder.

He headed back the way they'd come, then stopped short as he looked up at the sky over the inner courtyard.

Earlier it had been the blue of a fine summer day. Now it was mottled by storm clouds, moving fast, blowing across the patch of sky he could see.

In the dappled masses above him, shapes writhed, struggling to make their presence known.

You always saw shapes in clouds, he told himself, but this was different. These looked like demons trying to break through a barrier. And they weren't just the expected gray and white. Instead, as he watched, the colors turned vivid red like the sun had suddenly set on a tropical island. And then it turned dark, like a sudden storm was sweeping in. In the next moment, it was back to tranquil blue, before turning stormy again.

Lily made a strangled sound and pressed her shoulder to his. He put a protective arm around her, as though he could shield her from danger lurking above them.

Since he'd woken up in an unfamiliar bedroom, Mack had wanted to think he was in a real place. The sudden changes in the sky told him it couldn't be real.

"Don't you hear the music?" Roper asked.

Now that he mentioned it, there was a hint of music. Something classical, Mack thought.

"The Hall of the Mountain King," Lily whispered.

"What?"

"By Edvard Grieg."

"How do you know?"

"My parents liked classical music. My father had a CD of that."

"Okay."

"Where did all this come from—here?" Lily asked in a quavery voice.

"Here?" Mack asked. "Do you happen to know where we are?"

She gave him a startled look. "I was just speaking generally."

"Okay," Mack answered.

"Somebody's doing it," Roper said.

"That's impossible," she whispered.

Again Mack studied her. "Why is it more impossible than anything else?"

She swallowed hard, looking like she was trying to get a grip on herself. "I don't know. I just ..." She stopped and started again. "It's supposed to be the sky."

"So you expect it to follow the rules of the universe—as you know it?" Mack demanded.

"Yes."

"Apparently it's not true at the 'Hotel California'."

"The Hotel California?" Lily asked.

"As good a name as any," Mack shot back.

They all stood where they were, gazing upward until the clouds began to clear. The show was over quickly. In moments the heavens were back to rich blue.

"Normal again," Mack muttered. He looked back toward the hotel. "Maybe ... as long as I'm here, I'd better check on that guy—Jay Douglas—we left in the office," he said. "You all go back and ..."

"What guy?" Roper asked in a sharp voice, suddenly on alert.

"We don't know. When we first arrived, he attacked Lily. I tied him up. I want to see if he's okay."

"Attacked why?"

"I guess he became mentally unbalanced," Lily said.

"Why?" Mack asked.

"How would I know?" she answered.

"I don't like it," Roper muttered.

"You think we do? I'd better check on him."

Lily put a hand on Mack's arm. "Buddy system. I'll go with you.

"Right." He turned to Roper. "Will you report back to the others? About the sky?"

"And tell them what we saw?" the other man challenged.

Mack turned his palms up. "I hate scaring them. But I guess we'd better be honest. I mean, they need to be on the lookout for anything ... out of the ordinary—besides this whole setup," he added.

The insurance agent nodded tightly.

"We'll tell them about Douglas when we get back," Mack said.

Like Prospero in the Tempest, Danny Preston landed in the midst of a storm. Not on an island in the Atlantic but in the woods outside the Mirador Hotel.

He'd made the sky look weird and used some spooky classical music an elementary schoolteacher had played for her class.

And he'd dressed for his own pleasure as a biker, with a shaved head, leather vest, scruffy jeans and heavy black boots. His bare arms were covered with tattoos, serpents, dragons, and a death's-head dripping blood. A nice touch, he thought.

Although he'd talked a good game to the guy who had hired him for this job, he hadn't been perfectly confident that he could get here at all. Now he was elated at his success. Of course, he wasn't exactly in the hotel proper. He was in the woods on the other side of the wall that surrounded the manicured lawns and beautifully tended gardens. But he was going to get in there. Or lure some of the guests out here.

He'd always lived by his wits, and he came by his way of life honestly. His mom and dad had paid the bills as tag-team card sharks. That and pulling off some spectacular cons on puffed-up businessmen. Like the times they'd pretended that adorable little Danny had been injured on some company's property—then gotten a quick settlement to keep the supposed safety hazard out of the papers.

He'd outgrown that kind of risky stuff long ago. And he vowed he wasn't going to spend the rest of his life in federal prison like Mom and Dad. Which was why he was doing this job. Only, he didn't completely trust the guy who'd hired him, and when he was finished with the gig, he'd have to disappear.

The cell phone in his jean's pocket vibrated, and his face hardened. He'd just gotten here for Christ's sake. And Mr. Smith was already calling him. Yeah, Mr. Smith. Like that was going to fool anybody.

He let the phone vibrate for another few seconds before answering.

"Yeah?"

"Where were you?"

He was tempted to say, "Getting laid by the lake." Instead, he reported, "Getting the lay of the land."

"You're in?"

"Uh huh."

"Keep me posted."

"Let me do my work."

"We've got a deadline here."

"Then don't interrupt me. I'll call you when I have anything to report."

He hung up, annoyed that the guy was breathing down his neck.

He walked toward the wall at the edge of the hotel property. It had several wooden grillwork sections where he could look into the manicured grounds. And a door. As he turned the knob, it opened, but when he tried to push through, some kind of invisible barrier stopped him. It seemed that he had to stay out here, which meant he'd have to persuade one of the people on the grounds to come visit.

"Come on," he murmured. "I just need one of you to come over this way."

With Lily beside him, Mack turned and strode into the building, crossed the lobby and headed for the office where he'd left Jay Douglas tied up on the couch. When he opened the door and stepped inside, he took a moment to evaluate what he was seeing. The two phone cords and the masking tape were lying on the couch. So was the guy's clothing, but the man was missing.

Mack picked up the knit jacket of the running suit, then threw it down again.

When he heard a gurgling sound behind him, he pivoted.

Lily was staring at the couch as though it had turned into an open grave.

Mack gestured with his hand toward the phone cord, packing tape and pile of clothing on the sofa. "That's all there is, folks." He gave her a direct look. "What does it mean?"

"He could have taken off his clothes."

"How did he get untied?"

She shrugged helplessly.

Mack felt a surge of frustration. "Maybe he's Houdini. And maybe he's nuts. If he's on the loose, he could attack someone else. We'd better warn the others about *that, too.*"

Lily opened her mouth and closed it again. She had gone pale, and he saw she was pressing her hands against her sides, trying to keep them from trembling. But it wasn't working.

"Don't go freaking out on me," he said. "What do you know that you're not telling me?"

"Nothing."

She could be lying, but she looked so helpless that he reached for her. He'd held her in his arms after she'd been attacked, but he'd had to let her go to take care of the guy who was now missing.

As he gathered her close, she made a little moaning sound, and he felt chills rippling over her skin.

"What are you worried about?" he asked.

"Everything."

He sensed that she was a woman with a core of strength, which made her obvious distress all the worse.

She seemed to be completely out of her element in this weird environment. Shaken to her bones.

Maybe he was, too. At least he was in a situation he didn't understand. Like being tossed into a game arena where you didn't know the rules—or even the goal. But the human contact with the woman in his arms was like a balm to his own churning emotions.

He couldn't *do* anything about this confounding place or the strange events that kept cropping up. But he could *connect* with Lily Wardman.

He wanted to comfort her, to wipe away her fears. And outrun his own. Because in all his life, he had never encountered a situation where he didn't have some measure of control. His father had owned an outfitter business, and he'd taught his sons to be self-sufficient. There was always something you could do to help yourself, even if you were lost or injured in the middle of the woods.

But not here, it seemed, in this place where his memory stopped at an inconvenient point—then started again when he woke in the hotel room. Worse, he didn't know what was around the corner. One moment the sky was blue. The next, it was changing colors as if a kid with a crayon set had scribbled outside the lines. What was next?

He didn't want to speculate. Instead, he focused on the woman in his arms.

When she lifted her face to him, they stared at each other for a long moment full of tension. Not like the tension he'd felt in the bar. A more personal intensity.

Her hands gripped his shoulders. He stopped himself from running his hands up and down her back. There was something going on between them. Something that had flared to life almost from the moment they'd met.

Or was he making that up because she was the most appealing thing he had encountered here?

How did she feel about him?

In any other circumstance, he would have said she was attracted.

Here, he wondered if she only wanted the protection of a strong male who could fight off the terrors of a shifting environment.

He couldn't read her, probably because she was hiding something, but suddenly he couldn't cope with how much *he* felt.

The desperation of his own need was a shock. He wanted the woman in his arms. But he knew that physical attraction was only one component. He realized that he was also trying to prove that he was still the same man who had ejected from his plane.

And when was that?

Not yesterday. Days ago? Weeks?

He saw the look of regret in her eyes and wondered if her thoughts were similar to his.

"I'm sorry," he said as he eased away from her. Sorry that he wasn't pushing this further? Or that he'd let his imagination run wild when he'd embraced her?

He watched her take a step back and run a nervous hand down her side.

"It's this place," he said. "It's got us off-balance. And the guy disappearing doesn't help."

"I know," she agreed too quickly, then turned toward the door. "We'd better go back to the others."

"Right," he thought as he followed her out of the office. Safety in numbers. We won't have to worry about how to behave when we're not alone.

CHAPTER SEVEN

Lily kept her back to Mack as she struggled to regain her composure. She'd come close to kissing him. And that was absolutely the wrong thing to do.

He must be as confounded as she in a situation that was becoming stranger by the minute, yet he was dealing with it in a way that told her he had hidden resources she hadn't guessed at.

It was tempting to walk in his shadow, but she had to make her own decisions. Too bad she kept feeling like she was standing on a hill of sand that was shifting out from under her.

She'd thought she understood what she was getting into. Every time she turned around, some new surprise popped up like a demon in the dark corner of a fun house. Only in the fun house, you knew someone had put the shivery stuff there to scare you.

She'd been confident she knew the secrets of the place. But it turned out that she and everybody else had wandered into a backroom that wasn't on the blueprints.

Wishing she could talk to Phil Hamilton, the man who had sent her here, she dragged in a breath and let it out.

"Are you okay?" Mack asked.

Of course not. For so many reasons, but she gave him the only acceptable answer, "Yes."

Still, she couldn't face him yet. Her reaction to him was inappropriate, but not exactly a total surprise. She'd helped take care of him before they'd arrived here. Maybe he sensed that, because he'd asked if they knew each other.

She'd denied it, hating the lie yet knowing she couldn't get trapped into explanations.

Mack Bradley shouldn't be here at all, she'd told Hamilton, and he'd ignored her objections. Now she was even more convinced that this was a mistake.

Not just for Mack. For everyone. She didn't have the same personal feelings for them, but she knew too much bizarre stuff was cropping up. Stuff nobody had warned her about.

Or was that the point? Was she just as vulnerable as everyone else? And to what, exactly?

"What are you thinking?" the man beside her asked.

She dredged up a plausible answer. "About the guy who disappeared."

"Yeah, we'd better clue in the others."

"Tell them the truth?"

"As we know it."

Again, she gave the only response she could. "Okay."

"You had something else in mind?" he asked, his voice harsh in her ears. Probably he was trying to put some distance between them, pretend he hadn't pulled her close and held her in his arms, when they both remembered it vividly.

"No," she answered, wishing she were somewhere else. That didn't seem to be an option at the moment.

When they got back to the bar, she knew Roper must have described the cloud show in vivid detail because everyone was talking about it.

"Not like when the sun goes down or when a storm comes up?" Jenny Seville asked, looking toward her and Mack, probably hoping to get a different answer from someone besides Roper.

He scowled at her, his voice turning angry. "I *told you.* It happened too fast for any of that."

"I just want to make sure," she whispered.

Lily went to her and put an arm around her shoulder, feeling the young woman tremble. Wishing she had a better answer, she said, "Like the movie."

"But why?"

"We don't know."

When Mack cleared his throat, everyone looked toward him, and Lily knew he'd become the leader of the group.

"What?" Tom Wright snapped. The way he'd first strolled into the bar, he'd projected calm composure. Now his confidence appeared to be shredding around the edges.

"We need to deal with something else that happened," Mack said.

"Oh great," George Roper muttered. "Now what?"

"When we first arrived, Lily was attacked in the lobby by a man," Mack answered

As she expected, fear flickered around the room.

"What man?" Paula Rendell asked. "Where did he come from?"

"He said his name was Jay Douglas. I assume he was one of us."

"Was he wearing a running suit like we woke up in—or something else?"

"Running suit," Mack said.

"What else can you tell us?" Ben Todd asked.

"The only thing we know is that he was ... out of control."

"He wasn't a hotel staffer?" Paula asked.

"No. He sounded like an American. Maybe from the Midwest."

"And you don't know why he attacked? I mean—you didn't do anything to him?" she pressed.

"He seemed to be ... disturbed," Lily answered, wishing she could tell them that she was almost certain he wasn't coming back. But then she'd have to explain why she thought so. "Mack subdued him, and tied him up," she added. "Right before we met up with you, but when we went to check on him just now, he was gone."

"Gone where?" Ben Todd, the lawyer, demanded.

Mack shrugged. "I hate to keep saying we don't know. But it's true. My best advice is to keep an eye out for him—just in case he pops up again."

"Aren't we okay if we stick together?" Chris Morgan, the skier, asked.

"We can't just huddle in here," Mack snapped. "We need to find out more about this place."

"You mean go exploring, so we can get attacked?" Paula challenged.

"Or what if one of *us* disappears?" Jenny murmured.

"I don't think that will happen," Lily said.

"Why not?" Roper asked.

Mack tipped his head toward her. "Yeah, why not?"

Trapped, she shrugged. "Maybe I hope not," she said lamely.

"We'll keep using the buddy system," Mack answered.

"Fat lot of good that will do if there's another maniac—or the same one—lurking out there," Chris Morgan muttered.

"Or if someone's gonna disappear," Todd snapped.

Lily kept herself from offering anymore reassurances on that point.

Mack continued, "Every woman gets paired with a man."

"I'll go with you," Lily heard herself say. She'd been thinking that she and Mack shouldn't stay together, but she'd said just the opposite.

You can't get involved with Mack Bradley, she told herself. It will only end badly. Her heart squeezed. She had to distance herself from him. But that seemed beyond her current ability. Not when she was in the worst trouble she'd ever been in in her life.

The others paired up. Paula was with Roper again, like they'd been when she and Mack first encountered them.

Tom Wright, the car salesman, insisted on going alone which meant that Ben Todd, Chris Morgan and Jenny Seville made up the final team.

"You have any suggestions for how to divide up the territory?" Mack asked Paula.

"I remember the pool and tennis courts are out back and to the left," Paula said. "The spa's in the other direction. There should be a map of the hotel property."

"Where?"

She shrugged. "At the front desk?"

"What else do you remember?" Mack asked.

"The restaurants are mostly on this floor. And, of course, there are shops with expensive jewelry and saris you can take home."

"If we ever get home," Wright muttered.

"We'll look on the bright side," Chris Morgan answered.

They all chose a general direction.

Wright said he'd go upstairs and take the west wing. The Chris Morgan, Ben Todd and Jenny Seville team took the east wing.

Roper and Rendell would stay on the ground floor in the main part of the hotel.

"We'll meet back here in half an hour," Mack said, looking at his watch. "What time do you all have?"

Conveniently, everyone had a watch, and they were all set to the same time, which was four fifteen. Presumably in the afternoon, judging from the light.

When the others had departed, Lily scuffed her foot against the marble floor. "We could check out the guest rooms on the next floor."

Mack waited a beat before answering. "I don't think so."

She slid him a sidewise glance. He looked restless and hemmed in.

Without waiting for her to comment, he walked to the double glass doors, then along the covered passage to the lawn, where he stared at the manicured hotel grounds.

She followed his gaze. Everything seemed quiet and peaceful, but she sensed dark currents swirling just below the surface of what was obvious.

When he heard her follow, he asked, "What do you think? Can we get out of here?"

"I don't know."

"You sure you don't have inside information?" he asked with an edge in his voice.

"Why do you think so?"

"Your reactions."

"If you're saying I'm jumpy, everybody's jumpy."

He turned to look at her. "But you keep acting like you know what to expect. Then you're surprised when events don't follow the script."

Startled by his perception, she wanted to tell him there wasn't any script. Instead she settled for, "Am I?"

"Yeah."

She shrugged but couldn't meet his eyes. For a split second she wanted to ask him what to do about the strange things that kept cropping up, even when she knew that asking was out of the question. Plus, what did he know, anyway?

He let several seconds of silence pass before demanding, "Tell me some more about yourself."

"There's not much to tell," she said.

"Everybody has a story. Where did you grow up? Where did you go to school?"

"In the DC area. Bethesda."

"Your family was well off?"

"Yes. My dad's a lawyer."

"But you came to Baltimore."

"It's not that far away. I went to school there—Hopkins."

"They have a nursing school?"

"Yes."

"What do you do for fun when you're not working?"

She thought about that for a moment. What was she going to tell him—that she should have gotten married and had children the way her parents wanted, but she'd been too driven to make up for her families' sin? She settled for, "I haven't had much free time lately."

"Why not?"

"We're short staffed. I volunteered for double shifts."

"Did you get along with your family?"

She hesitated. "It wasn't always perfect."

"What was wrong?"

"My little sister got killed," she said, skirting around the real story.

"I'm sorry."

"Auto accident. What about you?" she asked, moving the subject away from herself. "You said you were from western Maryland. What did your parents do?"

"My mom was a housewife. Dad had an outfitter business. My brother took it over after Dad died. I graduated from the Naval Academy and went to flight school."

She already knew his background, but she was hungry to hear about his life—in his own words.

"You got along with your parents?"

"Yes. Mom had a business baking cakes and other stuff for people. Dad was pretty strict, but it was good for us."

"What happened to them? I mean you keep talking about them in past tense."

"They were on vacation in Paris and got caught in a terrorist attack."

She winced. "I'm so sorry."

"We had a good family life. It was over too soon."

When he didn't volunteer more, she said, "And you never married?"

His face hardened. "I was, but it didn't work out. I was away too much of the time."

"Sorry."

He lifted one shoulder. "Living on an aircraft carrier suits me. I work out in the gym. Read. Watch the movies they fly in. Go out on missions. The internet keeps me in touch with the world."

It sounded like an empty life, but maybe not more empty than hers. Was that part of what made him attractive to her? Two lonely, scared people reaching out to each other.

Maybe part. But from the moment she'd set eyes on him, she'd felt something for him.

When he started across the lawn toward the stucco wall that marked the boundary of the hotel lawn, her stomach clenched.

"Come back."

"I want to see what's in the woods."

Her hand shot out and grabbed his arm. "No!"

"Why does that idea frighten you?"

"It's outside the hotel grounds."

"So what?"

"You heard what Paula said."

"I don't trust *her* either."

"You're saying you don't trust *me?*"

He turned to look at her. "I want to. Should I?"

She longed to say, "Yes." She longed to tell him that she had his best interests at heart, but she couldn't get the word past her suddenly parched lips. When she'd taken on this part of the assignment, she'd been excited about a new adventure, but she hadn't been thinking about these people as individuals. Talking to them had changed her perception.

"You trust everyone here?" he asked.

"Why shouldn't I?"

"Why does Tom Wright want to go off alone? Is he waiting to contact someone?"

"Who?"

"I don't know."

"And I don't know where Paula got her information about this place."

"She's been here."

"Has she? And what's Jenny Seville hiding?"

"I don't know." She moistened her lips. "You're suspicious of everyone?"

"I have to be."

She wasn't exactly coming from the same place as he was. Still, now that she was part of the group, her stress level was off the charts, and her feelings for Mack Bradley were a big part of her roiling emotions. He interested her. Excited her. Inspired her admiration. She was even impressed by the way he wasn't taking anything at face value—even her.

He kept staring at her, and she managed not to look away.

Silent messages passed between them, messages neither one of them could acknowledge aloud. She stood her ground when she wanted to close the distance between them and grasp his shoulders.

The moment was interrupted by a creaking noise like rusty hinges. As they watched, the door in the wall opened—like an invitation.

CHAPTER EIGHT

Mack heard Lily suck in a sharp breath as she stared into the darkness.

As she stared at the open door, the expression on Lily's face was a mixture of panic and uncertainty.

When Mack started forward, she grabbed his arm. "Don't go out there."

"Why not?"

"Paula said it could be dangerous," she answered.

"Paula was talking about India. This isn't India."

"How do you know?"

"Too many weird things—like Douglas disappearing. The temperature being the same inside and out. The sky going wonky."

When he tried to tug away, she held fast.

"I want to know what's going on," Mack answered, unable to fight the sudden reckless impulse that grabbed him. "Is there something you know about this place that I don't?"

She hesitated for a moment, then whispered, "No."

"Then let's not waste this opportunity." Shaking off her hand, he charged toward the door in the wall.

Lily caught up with him and grabbed his arm again. "Stay here."

"I don't think so."

He felt the impatience bubbling like a boiler set to explode. It came from frustration with this whole out-of-kilter situation and from a compulsion he couldn't name—as though some impulse outside himself had taken control.

If he'd been thinking straight, that feeling of compulsion would have stopped him.

Instead he stepped through the open doorway into the woods. The light was suddenly dimmer, because the trees were blocking out the sun. There was no sound. No movement of the vegetation. If he was going to find out anything, he had to go farther in.

Mack started down a forest trail, leaving Lily behind. From the other side of the wall, the woods had looked normal. Now he saw that the tones were ... wrong, like when the sky had stopped obeying the laws of nature.

Pushing his way through thick blue vines with blood-red flowers, Mack broke into a forest clearing, but the trees around him were far from ordinary. This was some kind of enchanted forest. Did the gnarled trunks have faces with large staring eyes? He couldn't be sure. But the leaves were a rainbow of colors, changing and flickering like a rock concert light show. It was similar to the earlier changes in the sky, only now he was surrounded by it.

Far away in the depths of the forest he heard stirrings and strange calls. A huge black bird like the one they'd seen earlier emerged from the foliage along a branch and stared down with glowing red eyes, making a clacking sound with its large, curved beak.

Mack was focused on it, when a loud, roaring sound made him turn. A beast came charging out of the underbrush, headed straight for him. It had one enormous horn in the middle of its broad forehead, and it ran on short legs, heavy enough to hold up its armored body.

Dodging aside like a matador, Mack felt its hot breath as it went past and disappeared into a tangle of writhing red and orange vegetation.

That was the signal for all hell to break loose. Suddenly the woods were alive with branches swaying and the underbrush crunching. Sometimes he saw nothing but the foliage moving. Sometimes a strange-looking animal would leap out of the trees, heading for Mack or charging past him as though he weren't even there.

A series of savage growls made him spin to the right in time to see a troop of little men about three feet tall and dressed in animal skins emerge from the underbrush. Their faces were covered with warts, their hair was a matted mess, and they carried spears.

They looked at him and pointed. Then one screeched and threw his weapon, and the sharp tip dug into a tree beside Mack's shoulder. He pulled out the spear, and faced the attackers.

As he did, they all rushed toward him, screaming barbaric war cries.

He answered with his own furious shout as he threw the spear he'd pulled from the tree, striking the leader in the chest. The little man went down with a groan of surprise, and the others cried out in anger, launching their weapons. Mack snatched another spear from the ground and threw it back, taking down a second attackers.

If he ran, he'd be pursued by a hail of missiles. Choosing to stay and fight, he dodged behind a tree, scooping up a handful of spears as he took cover.

He swayed to the side, throwing, then dodging back as more missiles sailed toward him. When the volley stopped, he darted out and threw another couple of spears, keeping his eyes on the attackers, taking down another and another of the hoard. He might be outnumbered, but he was winning the battle. Finally, the remainder turned and fled.

When they were gone, he stood with his back against the tree trunk, breathing hard.

Where had the little warriors come from? Could they have killed him? Or was that just an illusion? And if so, what about the hotel and grounds on the other side of the wall? Was that an illusion, too?

Although he'd chased the ugly little men away, a terrible thought tore at him. If they were after him, were they after Lily, too? Could they kill her—because she'd followed him in here?

He'd left her somewhere in the woods. Now guilt and fear for her shot through him. If anything happened to her in here, it would be his fault.

Desperately, he shouted her name and thought he heard her answer from far away. But he couldn't be sure.

As he called her again, the trees around him began to shake in the kind of wind that precedes a violent storm. And while multicolored leaves flew through the air, he sensed something he'd been ignoring. A force was tugging at his mind, pulling out recent memories.

His temples throbbed in time to the pounding of the blood in his veins, and he moaned, hunching his shoulders and slapping his hands over his ears, but that did nothing to stop the awful whirling inside his head. He had to get out of here. Out of the woods. Back to the relative safety of the hotel grounds before every thought in his mind had been snatched away, and he was just an empty shell of a human body.

A noise from above made him look up. Standing on a tree branch, holding fast to the trunk, was a man with a shaved head and beard stubble, dressed like a biker. Although the forest shook around him, the tree where he stood remained steady, like a rock in the middle of pounding waves.

He was looking at Mack with clinical detachment, as though he was interested in how he was coping with this weird place.

"Are you doing this?" Mack croaked.

The man didn't answer.

"Make it stop!"

"No can do."

"I can't … think …"

"Sure you can. You are. Keep giving me information."

He started toward the tree, intent on climbing up and throwing the guy into the jungle. Before he reached the trunk, a voice stopped him.

It was Lily.

"Mack? Is that you, Mack?"

When he heard her, his heart leaped. Thank God!

"Lily! Where are you?" he shouted. As soon as he heard her voice, finding her became the total focus of his being.

"I don't know," she answered, her tone echoing the panic he felt.

"Keep talking."

"I ..."

"Sing something."

"What?"

One of his memories had been of Sunday school. "When the Saints come Marching Home. You know that one, don't you?"

"Yes." She began to sing the lusty old hymn.

Oh, when the saints go marching in,
Oh, when the saints go marching in,
Lord, I want to be in that number,
When the saints go marching in.

Her voice faltered at first, then grew stronger, and he followed the blessed sound. She didn't seem to know more than the first few lines, but she repeated them over and over. Listening to her helped him hang on to his sanity and his own memories as he staggered toward her. They crashed against each other in a clearing, and he wrapped his arms around her, rocking her in his embrace, so very thankful that he had found her and that she seemed to be all right. At least physically

He hugged her more tightly. "Lily, thank God. I'm so sorry I dragged you in here."

"You didn't drag me."

"Still my fault."

He noticed that she didn't argue about that. Still, she didn't say, "I told you so," as she clung to him.

Around them, the trees shook harder, making his head spin.

"We have to go back the way we came." He cursed in frustration. "But where?"

"There." She pointed behind him.

"How do you know?"

"I can see the light shining through the door."

He eased away and turned, seeing a rectangle of light shining through the foliage like a signpost, pointing toward safety. If they could only get there.

He ached to get the hell out of this death trap that seemed to be cobbled together from a random set of nightmares. But when he tried to move, his legs felt rooted to the ground, and he knew he wasn't going to make it out alive.

"Come on," Lily urged.

"I can't. You go on. Save yourself."

"No." She tugged on him, and he lost his balance, almost tumbling to the ground. The jarring motion was apparently what he needed. When she started pulling him toward the exit, he stumbled after her.

"Stay," the voice of the man in the tree boomed behind them.

"No," he answered, then raised his voice in defiance. "No."

"Then you'll be killed."

Lily gasped.

"You heard him?"

"Yes."

"Do you see him?"

She turned and looked back the way they'd come. Lifting her gaze, she looked toward the man in the tree, then quickly away.

"Come on," she urged. "The sooner we get away from him, the better."

"Both of you—stay!" His voice boomed the command like Zeus issuing a decree from Mt. Olympus. But whatever this guy was, he wasn't a god.

The warning only strengthened Mack's resolve to escape. Deep inside, he knew the man was lying. Mack Bradley's death was in here. And Lily Wardman's, too.

As they staggered toward the door, a huge animal rushed at them. Something bigger than an elephant, but with scales and fangs. Mack was sure they would be trampled by the truck-tire-sized feet or slashed to ribbons by the jagged teeth.

They kept running, the ground shaking from the impact of the beast.

Was the door moving farther away? Or was that just an illusion conjured by this place that didn't obey the laws of the universe as Mack knew them?

He put on a burst of speed, pulling Lily along.

With the animal almost on them, they dived through the doorway, tumbling out on the lawn where they lay panting.

The thing on the other side of the wall roared in anger. A huge eye peered out at them, but the behemoth was too big to get through the opening.

When the wall shook, Mack glanced back, praying that the monster wasn't going to crash through the barrier that separated safety from chaos.

But from this side everything looked different, the way it had before they'd gone in. Instead of fantasy shapes and colors, he saw only normal-looking trees.

With every ounce of strength he had left, he heaved himself up and staggered toward the door.

"Come back," Lily gasped.

"Gotta close it."

He slammed the wooden barrier closed, before staggering away from the wall again and sinking to the lawn beside Lily. She rolled toward him and gave a dry sob.

"It's okay. Everything's okay," he whispered, reaching for her and pulling her into his arms, clinging and rocking, so thankful that they had both escaped.

She clung to him, shaking.

"What happened to us in there?" she gasped. "I mean, everything turned crazy."

"Yeah, but we got out."

"Where did that loony stuff come from?"

"Loony." He laughed, then shook his head. "Yeah, Looney Tunes."

He had no real answers for her as he stroked his hands over her back, tangled them in her hair. He only knew that they were lucky to have escaped alive.

But they were safe now, and she was in his arms. He'd wanted to hold her like this, touch her like this. It had seemed wrong before. Now it was the only thing that felt right, as he focused on Lily instead of the terror in the forest.

What had happened in the forest didn't make sense. But they had escaped, and they could celebrate that.

They were both alive, and he needed to prove it.

The desperate look in her eyes undid him.

"That was impossible," she whispered. "It can't be real."

"Maybe not, but this is real."

He cupped the back of her head and brought her mouth to his. Perhaps in some part of his mind, he had intended it to be a reassuring kiss, but the moment his lips touched hers, he knew he wanted more.

Lily trembled in his arms, running her hands over his back, his shoulders, gathering him closer, melting against him.

He barely knew her. Or was that even true? He wanted to ask what they had been to each other. But he wanted to kiss her more.

She made a small, needy sound that sent sparks to every nerve ending in his body. He angled his head, first one way and then the other, greedy to give and take.

He lay back on the grass, pulling her on top of himself so that her body sprawled along the length of his.

With no conscious thought on his part, one of his hands slid down to her hips, pulling her lower body against his erection, knowing that would only make his craving for her worse.

But he was beyond rational decisions. Way beyond. He was all raw nerves and desperate feelings that the crazy trip through the woods had unleashed.

In this out-of-kilter environment, he'd been hanging on to the shreds of civilization as he knew it. He'd lost that veneer in the forest when they'd been running for their lives.

Needing more of the woman in his arms, he clasped her more tightly, pressing her breasts against his chest.

They had just escaped from dangers beyond his wildest imagining. Now he needed to affirm their escape—in this place where he couldn't trust his own observations or his senses—and where everything might change in an instant.

As they clung to each other, it was only a small leap to the next step. The need to claim her for his own, the need to be deep, deep inside her, erasing everything from existence except the two of them and what they could give each other.

He had forgotten where they were. Forgotten everything but the woman in his arms.

His hands stroked over her back, then down to her hips while he feasted on her, with an abandon that might have shocked him if he'd been capable of rational thought.

He worked his hand between them and cupped her breast, then glided his thumb across the beaded nipple.

Lord she felt so good, and the small sounds she made only fueled his passion.

He was about to pull up her shirt to give himself better access to her breasts when a bark of a laugh made them both go rigid.

CHAPTER NINE

"Is this what you consider exploring the hotel?" a voice said. "Looks like a more personal exploration to me."

Mack knew instantly that it was Tom Wright, the smart-ass car salesman.

Lily gasped and pushed him away, her face flaming.

Mack sat up and glared at the jerk intruder. He wanted to punch him in his grinning mouth but couldn't justify his outrage. He and Lily had been making a spectacle of themselves. But anyone else would have turned and walked in the other direction. They probably would never have known he was there.

Lily angled herself away from Mack. He saw her drag in a breath and let it out as she ran shaky fingers through her hair.

"Go back to the bar," he said to the man standing a few feet away. "We'll be along in a minute."

"Are you sure you can be trusted out here?" Wright asked, a sardonic note in his voice.

"Don't press your luck," Mack growled, making it clear that if the jerk stayed around, he was going to get hurt.

Wright shrugged and turned away.

Mack waited until they were alone, then turned to Lily. "I'm sorry."

"That will not happen again," she answered, punching out the words as she climbed to her feet and straightened her clothing. Without speaking again, she started jogging back to the hotel.

He didn't respond, because he would either be lying to her—or he would make her very angry.

Still he couldn't simply let her go. He needed to ask the question he should have asked when they'd first made it back to the hotel grounds.

"Wait a minute."

"No."

He caught up with her and put a hand on her shoulder. When she tried to shake it off, he said, "We have to talk about what happened in the woods."

She stopped, and he saw her face change when he asked, "In there—was something sucking at your mind—dragging out memories. And you couldn't stop it."

She clenched her teeth.

He squeezed her shoulder, then lessened the pressure when she winced. "This is important. Answer me."

'Yes."

"So that dog and pony show in there was designed to distract us—so he could do it."

She gave him a startled look. "How do you know?"

"I don't know for sure, but it's logical. I don't think he was just doing it for fun."

He kept his gaze on her. "And now? Did you lose those memories?"

She might not have understood what he meant, but her answer told him that she did. "I still have them."

"What exactly?"

"I'm not going to share private thoughts with *you*," she answered and started toward the hotel again.

But he wasn't willing to simply let her walk away. "Stuff from long ago—and recently?"

"Yes," she bit out without looking at him.

. . .

From his hiding place on the branch of a tree where he'd levitated earlier, Danny Preston watched the happy couple stride across the lawn as if a troupe of ugly little men were after them.

To be more accurate, Mack Bradley and Lily Wardman weren't happy and they weren't acting like a couple although they'd been about to fuck each other's brains out when the other guy had walked up and impolitely interrupted them.

What a dork. Unfortunately he was too far away for Danny to have gotten into *his* mind.

Of course, Danny had also watched the sexually charged performance with interest. He hadn't thought of himself as a sex therapist, but maybe he could sell his services to couples looking for a way to spark up their dull encounters.

He laughed, letting his imagination run with the idea for a few moments, then pulled himself back to the business at hand. His half-assed effects had lured Wardman and Bradley into the woods. With more time for research, he could have ginned up something from Hindu mythology that would go better with this place. But since he wasn't up on the subject, he'd settled for what he knew. Computer game images.

He'd used the distractions to get into their brains, while they'd been busy dealing with the threats he'd thrown at them.

Unfortunately, he couldn't dig deeply. But he knew that neither one of them was the person he'd been sent here to find and interrogate. Still, he'd eliminated two suspects. And he'd gotten some interesting information—particularly from Wardman.

Pulling out his cell phone, he punched the speed dial for one of his contacts. Not the guy named Smith. One of Danny's people.

"You okay?" his colleague asked.

"I'll be better when I know this thing is settled," he answered.

. . .

During his years in the CIA, Grant Bradley had learned never to take an unsolicited offer of help at face value. Which was why he knew he couldn't trust Colonel Jack Wilson.

No way was he walking into a twilight meeting with the colonel unprepared. The man might think that the drive to DC from Western Maryland would eat up the four hours before the rendezvous. Grant had other plans.

Starting with traveling light. As soon as he hung up the phone, he filed a flight plan, then checked out his Sig Sauer and slipped an extra clip into his pocket. His Cessna Skyhawk was in the hangar a few hundred yards across the landing strip from the house. He was in the air as soon as he'd gone through his flight check.

On the way, he thought about the layout of the meeting place. In addition to his wilderness outfitter business, he sometimes took small tour groups into the capital. If he had time, one of his stops was the Roosevelt Memorial.

He knew that the seven and a half acre site spread along the far side of the Tidal Basin was designed as a series of four outdoor rooms, each representing one of the thirty-second president's four terms. The "rooms" were divided by bushes, small trees and stone walls that would provide excellent cover for an ambush.

But not if Grant got there first.

Avoiding the flight restrictions over DC, he landed at a small airport in Laurel, Maryland, rented a car, and drove into town, where he found a parking space on the narrow road behind the National Gallery of Art. From there, he took a cab to the vicinity of the Roosevelt Memorial, arriving an hour and a half before the scheduled meeting.

There were still a few tourists in the area, and he mingled with them, scouting out the location and looking for signs that Colonel Wilson had already stationed someone here. But as far as he could tell, the only people here were visitors to the nation's capital.

When closing time neared and the Park Service officers began herding tourists toward the exit, he faded into the shrubbery, hunkering down until the area was clear.

Once he was alone, he climbed one of the artificial hills with a view of the entrance court and settled down behind a stone wall.

Twenty minutes after the Park Service rangers had left, two cars pulled up, and five men got out. Most looked young, with lean bodies and military short haircuts, wearing suits or sports jackets, presumably to conceal weapons. One of them had a fringe of dark hair surrounding a shiny dome.

After looking around the empty parking area, he called the group together for a conference. That had to be Colonel Wilson, if a colonel by that name even existed. Or maybe it was someone else entirely who had no connection with the U.S. government.

The leader moved cautiously toward the monument as his men fanned out around the area, except one of them who stayed with the Wilson character. His second in command or his bodyguard?

Grant studied their tense posture. It was clear this was no friendly meeting designed to reassure the grieving brother about Mack Bradley's whereabouts.

A flare of anger lanced through Grant. First he'd thought his brother was dead. Then a kind of cautious hope had surged through him. Now he didn't know what to think. Mack could still be dead, under circumstances that the brass didn't want to admit or reveal. Like that former football hero who had been killed by friendly fire.

Or he could be in secret captivity. By our side? Or the enemy?

Grant gritted his teeth, ordering himself to put his emotions aside. They wouldn't do him any good. Not when it was clear these guys were here to capture the nosy brother—or kill him to make sure his concerns about Mack Bradley went no further.

CHAPTER TEN

From his vantage point above the main tourist area, Grant watched the men take up positions around the monument, all of them facing the parking area. Their tactics confirmed his earlier assumption. It was clear that the team thought they had arrived first and were getting ready to give Grant a big surprise when he showed up.

Edging closer to the place where the leader of the operation was standing with his colleague, Grant strained to hear what they were saying.

"Do you think he'll show?"

"He wants to know what happened to his brother."

"Too bad he had to open that coffin. Who would have thought he'd do that?"

"Yeah, and if he finds out what's up, he'd better not be in shape to share the info with anyone else."

The pointed conversation confirmed Grant's assessment that there was never any intention of making this a friendly meeting.

He strained to hear more, but the colonel lowered his voice, sounding like he was giving commands into a microphone, sending his words to the earpieces of the men who were spread out around the area.

If Grant wasn't going to get any information from Wilson, who might or might not be working for the U.S. government, he had only a few alternatives.

64

Once again he surveyed the monument and the men who were settling in to surprise their quarry when he arrived. An excellent location for an ambush. Isolated and with ample cover.

The operatives faded into the underbrush, the way Grant had done earlier. But although they were concealed from the front, their backs were exposed. Like the French with the Maginot Line designed to repel a German invasion after World War I. All the guns faced East, with no way to swivel around.

He singled out the man who was closest to the Tidal Basin, and moved in that direction, avoiding detection as he zeroed in on his quarry.

The guy shifted his weight, his focus on the empty parking area, scanning for an approaching vehicle or perhaps someone on foot. Grant moved into position behind him, grabbed him by the throat and pulled him backwards. He used an illegal choke hold that would knock him out for a minute—or kill him if Grant had miscalculated. While the guy was out, Grant riffled through his pockets and took his wallet, which he slipped into his own pocket.

The guy was already stirring, and Grant grasped him by one shoulder and dug the barrel of his Sig into the man's back.

"Wha ...?"

"Take it easy. I just want information," Grant said. "What the hell is going on here—and with my brother?" he demanded, pretty sure that the guy didn't know the answer to the last part of the question. But he asked it anyway.

When the man didn't reply, he punctuated the question with a jab of the gun barrel.

"I said what's going on? Are you with the Navy?"

"I'm on assignment," he answered, ducking the question.

"To do what?"

The man hesitated for a fraction of a second. "To bring in Grant Bradley."

"Whose assignment?"

Before the guy could answer, Grant heard running feet and realized he had been too quick in his assessment of the situation. The guy wasn't just wearing an earpiece to receive orders from Wilson. He also had a mike, and the brief conversation had gone out to the rest of the men, who were now converging on Grant's location.

He stood up in the fading light, hauling the guy with him and using him for a shield as he faced the running men.

"Hold it right there, or your buddy gets it."

As they took in his words, the men stopped short about twenty yards from Grant and the unfortunate guy who'd gotten caught.

Confidently, the one he'd fingered as the colonel stepped to the front of the group. "Take it easy."

"Why the cloak and dagger setup?" Grant challenged as he took in the man's confidence. The guy had no doubt he was going to come out on top in this situation—which didn't exactly reassure Grant. Not to mention the guy Grant was holding who was now quivering in his grasp.

"We have to make sure you agree to keep your mouth shut."

"And if I don't?"

"That would be unfortunate," Wilson answered in a level voice.

"Tell me what's going on, and I'll make my own determination," Grant countered.

Several seconds passed before the colonel made a hand signal. Taking Grant completely by surprise, the other men began to fire the sidearms they carried, their bullets plowing into their comrade, who went limp in Grant's arms.

His only alternative was to return fire, forcing the attackers to duck away. He seized the opportunity to slip behind the gnarled trunk of one of the famous cherry trees that ringed the Tidal Basin. With nowhere to go but into the water, he dashed across the open space and dove in, ignoring the shock of cold and kicking downward, swimming away from the monument as bullets hit the water around him.

He had always been good at holding his breath, and he swam as far as he could away from the memorial before surfacing to grab a breath. When no bullets hit the water around him, he risked turning toward the shore where he plunged in. There were no figures standing on the pavement at the edge of the water, and he realized that they had cleared out, probably when they realized that their shots would have attracted attention.

He guessed they were in their cars, heading for the other side of the Tidal Basin. Lucky for him that there was no straight highway to the heart of DC. You had to follow a circuitous route through the park to get out of the Roosevelt Memorial area. Still, he picked up his pace. When he reached the far shore, he climbed a flight of steps, startling a guy leaning on the balustrade and dangling a fishing line in the water.

Grant ran a hand through his hair to get rid of the water, then headed for the tourist vans near the museums, thankful that some were still doing business.

As he stepped up to one of sellers, the guy eyed him with interest.

"You go for a swim?"

Grant lowered his voice. "Part of an initiation. If anyone asks for a wet guy, say you haven't seen me."

As he spoke, he kept himself from thinking about the brutal attack because his only focus had to be on getting the hell out of here in one piece.

He bought a dry tee shirt with a tastefully silk-screened picture of the Washington Monument and Jefferson Memorial and paired it with Bermuda shorts that were neon green, the least offensive ones that the vendor had left in stock that day.

He debated driving away in his wet clothes, then opted for not taking a chance on catching a cold.

After a quick trip into the bushes beside the Museum of Natural History to put on the dry clothing, he stuffed his wet slacks and shirt into a trash can, then hurried toward the car he'd rented.

He didn't feel like he'd made a clean escape until he was heading out of the city. As he drove, he was thinking he'd made a lucky escape and wondering what his next move was going to be.

CHAPTER ELEVEN

All eyes were on Mack and Lily when they rejoined the group. His gaze shot to Tom Wright, who was at the bar, smirking. Mack braced for a barrage of personal comments.

When none came he wondered if the jerk had decided there was no percentage in blabbing that he'd found them locked together in the grass.

Still, everyone was turned in their direction, expecting word of what had happened outside.

"You look shook up," Paula Rendell, the travel agent, said.

"Yeah," Mack acknowledged. He stalked to the bar, stepped behind it and pulled down a bottle of Jack Daniels. He poured a couple of fingers into a glass and was about to drink it down in one gulp. As it registered that everyone was still looking at him, he took a moderate swallow. It warmed his throat, but he didn't feel any immediate effect from the liquor.

When he glanced at Lily, he could see from her face that she expected him to do the explaining.

He took another hit of bourbon and said, "I recommend staying away from the wall that separates this place from the woods."

"Why?" Tom Wright, who had interrupted their public display of affection, demanded.

Mack set down the glass. "While we were out there, I was lured into the woods, and Lily followed me. Maybe I wouldn't

69

have escaped if she hadn't hauled me back through the door."

"Why wouldn't you have come out?" Jenny Seville, the teacher, asked in a small voice. Mack hated the fear he saw in her eyes, but at the same time he was glad she'd voiced the question. He'd expected her to wait for someone else to take the initiative.

"Because it felt like something had taken control of my mind. I was seeing all kinds of weird things that couldn't be real." Before anyone could press him, he went on to explain, "I felt a compulsion to go in there. And then a bunch of strange stuff started happening. Like I was attacked by three-feet-tall men carrying spears—and a large animal like a prehistoric beast chased us to the exit."

"Oh come on. Do you have a bottle hidden in the lobby or something?"

For the first time, Lily spoke up. "He's not making it up. I saw it too, and I assure you I haven't been drinking."

She looked like she was about to say something else but changed her mind.

"What?" Mack asked.

She dragged in a breath and let it out. "Okay, I was thinking that from here the forest looks normal. But when you get in there, the foliage can be any color. And all of the trees were shaking—except that one was staying still, and there was a man standing on a branch looking down at us— like he was the cause of it all."

"What did he look like?" Roper demanded.

"He had a shaved head, and he was dressed like a biker. He was telling us that we'd be killed if we tried to leave the woods, only I was pretty sure it was the other way around. If we stayed there, we'd end up dead."

She stopped talking abruptly, looking like she was astonished at how much she'd revealed about the incident. Or maybe she was finally coming to grips with what had happened to them in the forest.

"Thank you. We needed to know that," Paula Rendell said in a reassuring voice.

Chris Morgan gave her a sharp look. "Why, exactly?"

"Isn't it obvious?" Ben Todd asked, sounding like he was badgering a witness in court. "So we can avoid the same thing happening to us."

"Can we?" George Roper demanded. "I mean, if shit like that can pop up out of nowhere, what's to stop *any old thing* from happening?"

"So far there's been nothing like that in the hotel," Mack said.

"Doesn't mean it can't," Roper countered.

"Let's hope not," Ben Todd, interjected. "I'd like to know there's somewhere we can count on being safe."

Although Mack understood the sentiment, he wasn't willing to count on it. Still, he nodded in agreement. Nothing wrong with hoping.

"How did you get out of the woods?" Paula asked.

"We fought our way out."

When someone winced, he modified the observation. "Well, not exactly fought," he said, thinking about the pitched battle with the spear carriers, which he didn't mention. "An elephant-sized animal with scales and horns charged us, and we made it through the door in the wall. He was too big to get through."

When Mack stopped talking, there were several moments of silence as that last piece of information sank in. Ben Todd finally said, "That's quite a story."

Mack shrugged. "I know it sounds fantastic, but it's what happened. I'm not making it up."

"I wish we were," Lily said in a barely audible voice.

"So stay away from the woods," Mack repeated what he'd said earlier. He glanced around the room, hoping he was getting silent agreement from everyone.

"I'm staying right here," Jenny Seville said, confirming his assumption about her as she looked around at the rest of the hotel guests like she hoped others were going to keep her company.

Paula and several of the men nodded in agreement. Mack noticed that Lily wasn't signing up for the group sit-in.

Neither was Tom Wright, the car salesman. "I've had enough of other people telling me what to do. I think we're okay if we stay in the hotel."

"Based on what?" Mack asked.

"Maybe because that's what I fucking well *prefer* to think," Wright said, his voice rising as he spat out the words.

"Keep your comments civil," Paula said.

"Why should I?"

Lily shook her head. "Because it's better to be polite. Foul language can only make things worse."

"How could they be worse?" he shot back.

Mack waited for her answer, but she didn't offer any insights.

George Roper stood up, walked to the back of the bar and snatched a bottle of Dewar's from the shelf. He poured himself a tumbler full and held it up to the light, looking at it like the secret to the "Hotel California" might reside in its amber depths.

"If I drink all the Scotch here, do you think there will be more in the morning?" he asked.

It was a very interesting question, but nobody had an answer.

"If we all just sit here, we're going to get on each other's nerves," he said, shooting Jenny a look.

"What do you suggest?" Ben Todd asked.

"Each of us could write down what we're feeling," Lily suggested.

That drew several derisive laughs from the men in the room. "You want to turn this adventure into a therapy session?" Tom Wright asked, his tone mocking.

"I guess not."

"Is it an adventure?" Todd asked.

Roper made a disparaging sound. "Like being dropped in the middle of Disney World with no cast members to tell you what to do."

Again Mack watched Lily, trying to gauge her reaction. She didn't seem to like the comparison.

"Nobody else reported what they found," Jenny said, sounding hopeful.

"That's right," Lily quickly agreed. What was she expecting? Some revelation, or was she seeing the exchange as a way to pass some time? And then what?

"Well?" Mack asked. "Did you find anything we should know about—or anything particularly interesting?"

The other teams gave reports. Nobody had found anything besides a luxury hotel—with an abundance of upscale facilities. But no staff members in the place. The only unusual trip had been into the woods, and Mack was thinking they could have avoided it if they'd just stayed where they were supposed to be.

Supposed to be? He wondered what that meant exactly.

"I've got a question," Paula said. "Was the—unpleasantness—in the woods designed by the management to keep us in the hotel? Or was it an outside influence?"

"Good question," Mack said, looking at Lily. "Outside influence or part of the setup?"

"How would I know?" she shot back.

He shrugged. "Just trying to get your opinion. Do you have one?"

"Outside influence," she finally said.

"Why do you think so?"

She was ready with a quick answer. "Because there's nothing to be afraid of in here."

"Except the guy who tried to choke you," Mack reminded her.

"But he's disappeared."

"Has he?"

"I hope so," she answered quickly, and again he couldn't help thinking that she knew more than anybody else.

When she didn't volunteer anything else, Mack looked at Roper, who had made the comment about the liquor to the group in general. "Anybody sleepy?" he asked.

They all considered the question. Nobody answered in the affirmative.

"Here's another one. Anybody have to go to the bathroom?"

Again nobody was feeling a full bladder.

"And we're all in tip top physical condition?" Mack asked.

He watched the people in the room taking inventory. Some stood up and stretched. Others raised their hands above their heads or bent over and reached down toward their toes. Jenny turned her head from side to side.

"I had a stiff shoulder," Todd said. "It's better now."

"Yeah, and my knee isn't giving me any problems," Paula reported.

"That's all good, isn't it?" Lily said.

"Hopefully," Mack answered.

"You don't want to feel good?"

"Sure I do. But the last thing I remember is ejecting from a fighter jet. You'd think I'd have some aftereffects? At least some muscle pulls or something? Do you have a medical opinion about that?"

"A medical opinion?"

"You're a nurse, aren't you?"

"Yes."

He thought he saw a shadow cross her face, but it was gone before he could be sure it was really there.

"So let me ask the sixty-four-thousand-dollar question," Mack said. "Now that we've been here awhile and thought about our physical condition, where do you think we are?"

He saw various reactions around the room.

"A prison?" Chris Morgan muttered.

"Why do you think so?" Ben Todd asked him.

"Because we can't get out."

"If it's a prison, it's pretty plush."

"How about a mind-control experiment?" Todd asked.

Jenny winced. "Do you really think so?"

"It's as good a guess as any."

At the side of the room, Tom Wright stood up, and Mack looked toward him.

"You have a theory?"

"Not that I want to discuss."

"But you're thinking something," Mack pressed.

"I'm thinking I've had enough cheerful togetherness," the man clipped out. He headed for the door, then stalked out of the room. Mack waited for several moments, then stepped into the hall, seeing the defector striding toward the lobby. He followed, staying near the wall and several yards back as he watched the man stalk across the expanse of marble floor and turn right into the main hallway. Wright marched into the business center and closed the door behind him.

Mack walked quietly to the door, pausing at the side of a potted palm, and waited several seconds to let Wright think he was alone. Finally he eased the door open a crack and looked in. The car salesman was seated at one of the computers. He turned it on and waited. Mack held his breath. Did this guy know something that the rest of them didn't? Like did he have a way to communicate with the outside world? Long seconds passed, and then a message flashed on the screen, "Unable to load mail."

"The fuck you say. I mean, what is this?"

Wright slapped the desk next to the machine, then began pressing buttons. The tactic didn't produce a mail program, but the screen flashed with an announcement of games and movies.

"Oh right," Wright muttered. "Canned stuff. Just what we need to keep us occupied."

Mack might have stepped into the business center, but movement at the corner of his eye caught his attention. He stayed still, facing the door, but he swiveled his eyes in time to see Lily climbing the stairs. She looked like she was in a hurry—with a known destination in mind. Maybe following her was more productive than trying to figure out what Wright was up to.

Mack eased farther behind the palm, watching Lily pause at the top of the stairs and scan the lobby. She had gotten out of the bar pretty quickly. He'd like to know what excuse she'd made to the others, since they'd already established that nobody had to go to the bathroom or were tired.

As he watched, she headed down the hall. He waited again, then made a dash up the stairs, noting that he could run up the flight without feeling winded.

When he turned in the direction she'd gone, the hall was empty, and he clenched his fists in frustration. Then he remembered she'd said she was in room 250. It could be a lie, but the way she'd said it argued for its being the truth.

He moved along the carpet, stopping at room 250. He could have knocked. Instead he tried the knob. It was locked, and he felt a surge of disappointment. And also surprise at his own actions. Since when did he walk into a woman's bedroom unannounced? And without an invitation.

He could have turned and gone back to the bar, but he had the conviction that finding out what Lily was up to was more important than anything else he could think of.

Why? He couldn't answer. Yet he couldn't shake the feeling that everything in here was speeding up and that if he didn't find out what was going on, time would whiz by so fast that it would smack him in the ass on the way past.

Not even sure what that meant, he stared at the lock. Then, on a hunch, he slipped the keycard out of his pocket and inserted it in the door slot. As he'd half expected, the light turned green. And why not? It was kind of like the computers not giving access to personal mail but providing a selection of games and movies.

Fake. Or not designed to function the way you had a right to expect.

A right?

He was pretty sure his rights had been summarily snatched away from him before he'd woken up in this artificial environment. Because he knew it was only a cunning shadow of reality. And maybe it would have taken longer to figure that out if the sky hadn't turned wonky and the guy in the woods hadn't tried to take over his mind. His only consolation there was that the same thing had happened to Lily, too. She hadn't been faking her fear and confusion. In fact, maybe it was worse than his, because she expected something from this place—and wasn't getting it— and he had no expectations.

Quietly he pushed the door open and stepped across the dark polished wood floor onto the plush Oriental rug, feeling the thumping of his heart. Because he was doing something he knew was wrong? Or because he thought he was finally going to get some information?

He spared the chamber a quick glance. Like his digs, this was a suite with a living room furnished in English period pieces and presumably a bedroom down a short hall.

He might have moved slowly and quietly, but he was in a hurry now. Good thing. As he strode down the hall, he saw Lily reaching for the closet door. When she realized she wasn't alone, she pushed the door shut, her eyes wide as she stared at the man who had dared to follow her into what should be personal space.

"What are you doing here? You don't just walk into a woman's bedroom," she said in a voice it seemed she couldn't quite hold steady.

He'd had the same thought before he'd decided to follow through on the forced entry. Well, not exactly forced.

"How did you get in?"

He held up the plastic rectangle. "With my keycard."

"Your card? Why would it work in my door?"

"Because the locking system is fake, just like the entertainment system is all old, prerecorded stuff."

Before she could grapple with that, he shot another question at her. "Why did you rush up here?"

"I didn't rush."

"You looked like you were in pretty much of a hurry when I saw you race up the stairs."

"But I checked ..." Her voice trailed off as she must have realized what she was admitting. She started again. "What were you doing, following me?"

He lifted one shoulder. "To be clear, I was following Wright, not you. I was at the door to the business center when you flew past. What was so important that you left the rest of those wretched souls to fend for themselves?"

"I'm not their keeper."

"What are you?"

She hesitated for a moment. "A person who ended up in this weird place."

"I think you know more about it than the rest of us."

"No."

The denial lacked conviction.

CHAPTER TWELVE

Lily didn't like the accusatory tone of Mack's voice. It was one of the many things she hated about this whole miserable charade. Not just that he'd asked the question but that she had to keep him from finding out what she'd been going to do.

She might have screamed in frustration, if that had been an option. When she'd agreed to put herself in this situation, she hadn't understood all the implications. Not by a long shot. Before she'd woken up in her bedroom in the Mirador Hotel, she'd thought of most of the other people who were here in the abstract. With the exception of a few, like Mack Bradley. Now she could see that they were real individuals with real problems and real fears.

But her change of perception wasn't just having to do with the people she'd met here. It was the black bird that had landed in the woods, the clouds that had taken over the sky, turning the bright blue into a preview of horrors to come.

And then going into the woods with Mack and almost losing her mind. If he hadn't been with her, she was pretty sure she would have ended up like someone who'd had a prefrontal lobotomy.

Now he had invaded her bedroom with an aggressive defiance that would have frightened her if he'd been one of the other men in the hotel.

But this was Mack, the only guy here she thought she understood. In the short time they'd been in this place, she'd seen him as a born leader, a protector of the weak, and also a man who was determined to figure out why he had ended up with a bunch of strangers in this hotel.

And when he'd decided she was acting suspiciously, he'd wanted to know what was up.

As he moved purposefully toward the closet, she knew she had to keep him from going in there. And the only way she could think of was to make him change the focus of his thoughts to something a lot more personal than Lily Wardman's suspect motivations.

Without giving herself time to reconsider, she reached for him.

The move was so out of character that she could hardly believe what she was doing. She hadn't been with a man in years. She certainly shouldn't be with this one. But something about this place and the man made it seem like the right thing to do, at least at this moment.

And she had a good reason, she told herself. She had to stop his blatant snooping.

Of course it was a lot more than that. She'd been drawn to him, not just when she'd encountered him in this weird environment. Before ... .

Well, she'd better not think about that. As far as this reality was concerned, there was no "before." There was only now.

As she folded him into her arms, she felt him go very still, probably trying to decide how to react to her sudden invitation.

Even as she drew him closer, she knew deep down that it was the wrong thing to do, and perhaps in some part of her mind, she was hoping he would break the contact.

He'd come in here to challenge her. But it seemed that she'd succeeded in making him forget his reason for being in her room, and she was having a similar reaction. As he moved to gather her close, any hesitation she felt was simply blotted out the way strong sunshine strikes a windshield and temporarily blinds you.

Mack Bradley filled her senses as he lowered his mouth to hers in a kiss that took up where they had left off out on the grass. Both of them had been powerfully aroused not long ago, and now that arousal fused them together as though the physical separation during the time they'd spent in the bar afterwards had only been a way of increasing their need for each other.

Part of her mind still knew that this personal contact was wrong in so many ways, but she was beyond heeding anything besides her own needs—and his. If she could give him nothing else, she could give him herself. At least for this small space of time.

He angled his head, drinking from her like a man who had been stumbling across a desert, sure that he was going to die—then finally finding the one thing that would keep him alive.

And she silently admitted that the kiss was no less potent for her. She drank him in, tasting the bourbon on his breath and also the need. She knew he'd been alone for a long time. She knew from poring over his biography that it wasn't easy for him to let down his guard, but here he was clasping her to him, running his hands up and down her back, cupping her bottom as he drank her in with an urgency that made her own needs rise to meet his.

When he pulled away, she heard a sob of protest rise in her throat, but he was only giving himself the space to yank the tee shirt he wore over his head. She did the same with her own shirt and bra, discarding them and tossing them away.

She and Mack were both naked to the waist, and she fought the impulse to cross her arms across her breasts as his scorching gaze traveled over her, making her nipples tighten to hard points.

"You are stunning," he growled.

Nobody had ever said that to her.

"Am I?"

"Oh yeah." As he spoke, he reached for her again, pulling her close.

She gasped at the skin to skin contact, her nails digging into his naked back. She could feel his erection pressing against her through the fabric of his jeans and her trousers.

He muttered a low curse, and she knew he was thinking the same thing she was. The rest of their clothing was in the way.

She found the button at the top of his jeans and opened it before reaching to open his fly. He was doing her the same favor, dragging her pants down and out of the way. When they were both naked, they clasped each other, exchanging hot kisses.

He filled her senses, taste, touch and the rough sound of his voice as he whispered hot, erotic words.

Lifting her up, he carried her to the bed, laying her down gently, his gaze roaming over her. She stared up at him, admiring his strong body and the thick erection that stood out in front of him.

"And you are breathtaking."

She flushed when she realized she'd said that aloud.

"Oh yeah?"

"Oh yeah," she echoed as she clasped her hand around his cock, feeling the weight and the power of him.

His gaze burned into hers as he watched her stroke him.

"Don't make me wait," she murmured.

He answered with an inarticulate sound, coming down beside her on the bed and sweeping her into his arms. Their legs tangled together as they rocked in each other's arms, hands stroking, mouths seeking and finding. He rolled her to her back, and she opened her legs for him, clasping him again so that she could guide him into her.

When they were joined, he went very still, poised above her as though he were committing every detail of this moment to memory.

Then he began to move, a few slow strokes that quickly turned to a fast rhythm that she strove to match as they both drove up a steep incline. When they reached the top, they flew off the edge together, clinging to each other as sensation swept through them.

For a few moments they had been somewhere else. She didn't even know where. Then she heard his harsh breathing, felt his weight settle.

He raised his head, staring down at her, before rolling to his side, taking her with him.

For long moments, neither of them spoke.

Finally he said in a gritty voice, "I'm sorry. You didn't exactly invite me into your bedroom."

"It worked out okay," she answered, wondering when sex had ever been that shockingly powerful.

"The thing is, we haven't even had a first date."

"Are you having regrets?" she heard herself ask.

"Probably that should be my line."

She shook her head. "Neither one of us was prepared for what that trip into the woods did to us."

He stroked his hand up her arm. "Yeah."

"Has anything like that ever happened to you?" she asked.

"No, you?"

"No."

Her skin had been flushed. Now the cool air was uncomfortable. When she reached for the edge of the spread, he climbed out of the bed so that he could pull the covers down before getting back under and covering them both. She moved back toward him, and he turned on his side so that he could gather her close.

Neither of them spoke again for a while, and she wished they could just drift here, calm and peaceful in the afterglow of making love. She didn't want to think too much about what they had just done, or why. Or what might come next. Logically, making love with him had been an act of madness, because nothing could come next she told herself.

He caught the shiver that went through her.

"What?"

"I was thinking about this place," she said, not exactly lying, she told herself.

"You mean, that we both grabbed the opportunity to get away for a little while."

"I hate to put it that way," she whispered.

"How would you put it?"

"We're both feeling shaky—and we turned to each other."

"Okay."

She didn't love the way he'd said that. But she wasn't going to challenge him on his feelings.

"I don't usually ..."

"Hop into bed with a guy you hardly know," he finished for her.

"Yes," she agreed. "How do you know?"

He laughed. You are definitely not that kind of woman.

"What kind am I?"

"What they used to call a good girl. Casual sex isn't part of your morality."

She answered with a small nod. "And you're a guy who spends long periods away from home. And when you're on leave, you ... tend to let your hair down."

"We wear our hair short."

"I meant figuratively." She found his hand under the covers and wove her fingers with his. "So tell me about Mack Bradley."

Again, she'd read his file and knew some of the basics. But she wanted to hear more of what he chose to tell her.

"I already said some stuff downstairs."

"Yes," she answered. "I know what you do and the last thing you remember before waking up here. But what do you think is important about yourself?"

He thought for several moments. "I don't know. I had a pretty normal childhood in western Maryland. And I think I was lucky having a lot of freedom to just be a kid. Probably the most unusual thing about me is that I have a twin brother."

"Were you friends or rivals?"

"Friends. And sometimes rivals. I think we both made an effort not to end up in exactly the same place. I went to the Naval Academy. He went to McDaniel College, then joined the CIA."

"He's still with them?"

"He left to work for a private security agency. Then he went back home to run our dad's outfitter business."

"He hasn't settled down?"

"Neither have I." He made a dismissive sound. "Well, I was married but it didn't work out."

"Why not?"

"I think she started off seeing my job as glamorous. Then she didn't like the long separations. After she left, I focused on my career. Maybe I was trying to prove to myself that any sacrifices I made were worth it." He snorted. "And now I'm *here*, which means that anything I was doing before this is …"

"What?"

He lifted one shoulder. "I don't know. Did you ever watch Twilight Zone reruns?"

"Yes. My mom and I watched them together."

"And a lot of times people were trapped in some kind of some kind of meaningless existence."

"Why bring that up?" she asked, wishing she could soothe away his doubts.

His face hardened. "Because you know as well as I do that this place isn't real."

She opened her mouth to protest, then closed again as he kept talking.

"Maybe I could have convinced myself it was—at least for a while. But not after that crap with the sky—and then the woods. It's like being on an LSD trip, only we weren't imagining it. Were we?"

"No," she whispered.

"What are the chances of getting out of here, do you think?"

She swallowed around the sudden lump in her throat. She wanted to assure him that, of course, they were getting out, but she knew it was almost certainly a lie.

She saw him studying her. "What?"

"What are you worried about?"

"The same thing as you."

Although he didn't comment, she wondered if he believed it.

Instead, he said, "Your turn."

"To what?"

"Tell me something about yourself."

"Like what?"

"Like why did you become a nurse?"

She swallowed hard, thinking that she would have phrased the question differently.

"Because of my little sister," she answered. "When she was five, we were in an auto accident. She had refused to sit in her car seat, and she was thrown from the car. My dad was driving, and he said it was his fault that he hadn't insisted on strapping her in." She stopped and took a breath. "She was in a coma, and there was nothing they could do for her. The doctor wanted to pull the plug, but Dad insisted on keeping her on life support."

"I thought you said she was dead."

That's what I usually say—so I don't have to explain the rest of it. Really, she's still alive. Well, her body is alive. She's in a vegetative state." She stopped talking abruptly, fighting the tears blurring her vision.

"That's rough," Mack said, stroking his hand up her arm.

"Uh huh," she answered, still struggling to get her emotions under control.

"I guess your family is rich," he said.

Her head jerked up. "Why do you think so?"

"You can afford to keep her in a hospital bed. That has to take money."

She nodded. "My parents are well off, but not exactly rich. Dad's set up a special trust fund to take care of Shelly."

"How old is your dad?"

"In his seventies."

"So he won't be here forever to insist on your sister's treatment. And then you'll have to decide what to do."

"Unfortunately."

"Why do you put it that way?"

"I used to be very clear about what I thought. Somehow it's gotten harder over the years—not easier."

He nodded.

"Listen, I'm exhausted. Do you mind if I take a nap?" she asked.

"I thought nobody got tired here."

"Maybe it's emotional exhaustion."

"Yeah. Or maybe they flip a switch, and everyone suddenly has to sleep."

"Is that what you think?"

"I guess we'll find out."

"I guess," she agreed, not knowing what else to say.

When she eased down in the bed, he stayed beside her, and she wished there were some way to tell him that she was feeling the effects of too much intimacy. She'd focused on her career for a long time. Being with Mack made her realize that maybe she'd been too quick to give up ... what? Marriage and a family? She'd always told herself she could do without those things. Now she wondered why she'd been so willing to set them aside. Was she like Dad—feeling guilty that she had survived the car crash with hardly a scratch, and Shelly had lost everything?

. . .

Paula Rendell looked toward the stairs. Mack Bradley and Lily Wardman had been gone for a long time. Maybe they'd gone to one of the bedrooms to talk, but Paula didn't think so. She'd always been good at reading people, and she was pretty sure the two of them were attracted to each other. She got the feeling that Tom Wright had found them in a compromising position outside, although he hadn't said much—only thrown some broad hints. And then the couple had gone up stairs, which she could view as keeping them out of trouble.

Her attention was refocused when a nearby door opened and, speak of the devil, Wright came out, his face a classic picture from one of those TV commercials where a poor jerk learns he's been doing something all wrong. In the next scene, he's going to find out the magic product to solve his problem—like a special machine that works much better than crunches to flatten his stomach. For three easy payments of $9.99. Only Paula suspected that there wasn't going to be an easy solution for Wright—or anyone else who had ended up in the Mirador Hotel.

When Paula started toward him, his head jerked up, and she was pretty sure he hadn't wanted to be seen coming out of the business center. Interesting.

"Something wrong?" she asked.

"I ... I need to contact my wife."

"You have a wife?"

"Yeah."

"You don't seem like the type."

He shrugged. "We had a fight. I want to make sure she's okay."

Paula nodded, wondering if that was the real story. "And the computers and phones aren't working?"

"Yeah."

With a quick shake of his head, he turned and strode away.

CHAPTER THIRTEEN

Like a felon behind the wheel of the getaway vehicle after a bank heist, Grant drove with one eye on the rearview mirror. But he kept his speed below the limit as he headed away from the scene of the crime. Not his crime, he reminded himself. Now that he was in the car and driving away, it was impossible not to flash back to the impact of the bullets hitting the man he'd been holding up as a human shield. He'd thought there was no way the colonel's men would shoot one of their own. He'd been dead wrong—although he was the one who had gotten away, leaving a bloody corpse in the shrubbery. And now that he'd made his escape, he had time to reflect on just how ruthless and brutal the attack had been. All Grant had wanted was information about his missing brother, and they'd gone to unimaginable lengths to make sure he didn't get it.

Christ, what was going on here?

As soon as he'd opened that coffin and found the dummy inside, he'd known in his gut that something sinister was in play. He'd wanted to convince himself that there was some legitimate explanation. Now that was impossible—not after the ambush at the memorial and the hail of bullets. But, odd as it seemed, the way things had gone down gave him a tiny spark of hope.

Mack could still be alive, being held captive. But for what purpose? Like did he have some piece of information that would help a group of jihadists or something? The colonel

90

had sounded like an American, but couldn't that be true of a terrorist?

As he thought about the fierce attack again, Grant fought the urge to get out of sight by pulling into a downtown parking garage. But he couldn't do it because, if they had already spotted him, he'd be trapped. Instead, he kept driving just below the speed limit and headed for upper Connecticut Avenue. A few blocks from Chevy Chase Circle, he turned off onto one of the residential side streets and pulled up under a line of mature trees along the curb. Leaving the engine running, he retrieved the dead man's wallet from the glove compartment and riffled through the compartments.

There was about five hundred dollars in cash, but no credit cards and no ID.

Cursing under his breath, he started pulling up leather flaps and found a Maryland phone number. Just the number. No name or clue about where it was located. But Frank Decorah had allowed him to keep his password to the Decorah Security database, and Grant had left his laptop under the driver's seat.

When he pulled it out and put in the phone number, he found it came from a facility called Hamilton Labs. And when he did some further poking around, he gathered that the place was a hush-hush biotech company.

What did that have to do with Mack Bradley? Could his brother actually be there?

Grant fought to quash the surge of hope bubbling up inside himself. It could be that the number was totally unrelated to the Mack Bradley case. But that seemed unlikely, since the operative had taken all the identifying evidence out of his wallet except this one piece of contact information.

The only way Grant was going to find out anything was to go there. And put his life in danger again?

Yeah, because that was the only lead he had.

But when he started to shove the paper with the phone number into his pocket, he realized he was wearing the pair of Bermuda shorts and tee shirt he'd just bought. His next stop was a discount department store where he bought a dark tee shirt and pants plus clean underwear, shoes and socks. No point in squishing around in wet footwear when you were sneaking up on guys who wanted to kill you.

It gave him some satisfaction to use money from the dead guy's wallet to pay for the purchases. Then he returned to his car and took the spare handgun out of the trunk.

Lily tried to relax, but she could feel the tension building inside her as if a little man were sitting at a control panel inside her and relentlessly messing with her vital signs.

Mack turned his head toward her. "What?"

She swallowed hard. "Like I said before, this is all moving pretty fast for me. Are you going to be ... angry if I say I need some time alone?"

"By 'all'—do you mean the mystery of the Mirador Hotel? Or our ... relationship?"

"Everything," she said in a small voice.

"Okay." Pulling the covers aside, he stepped out of bed and began picking his clothing off the floor. He was dressed in his jeans and tee shirt in under a minute.

"I can meet you downstairs in a while," he said.

She felt instantly guilty for effectively kicking him out— and feeling relieved that he was willing to give her some space.

"Yes. Good," she answered, hoping she sounded more casual than uptight. "Probably we don't want to come down together and give everyone something to talk about."

Before he left, he looked toward the window. "Does it ever get dark here?" he suddenly asked.

"What?"

"Does it get dark here?" he repeated.

The question took her by surprise, but she managed to answer, "How would I know?"

He shrugged. "Just trying to figure the place out."

Did she even know the answer? She'd thought she would only be here a few hours and that she would keep her interactions to a minimum. That plan hadn't worked out quite the way she'd assumed, and now every second in the hotel had started to weigh too heavily on her.

She waited with her heart pounding as Mack walked down the hall to the living room, then exited the suite. She sat up, counting to a hundred to make sure he wasn't going to come back. Finally she climbed out of bed and pulled on her panties, bra and blouse. There was really no point in getting dressed, but she didn't want someone—Mack—to find she'd gone with half her clothing still here. As she pulled on her slacks, she wondered what he was going to think when he found out she wasn't in the hotel.

Standing beside the bed, she clenched her hands into fists, feeling trapped and wishing she'd planned this whole thing better. When Mack figured out she'd vanished, he'd be angry. And hurt. Could she come back and explain who she was and why she'd come here? Or would it already be too late?

She looked toward the living room. She'd like to lock the damn door, but she'd already found out that wouldn't do her any good. And if she dragged a chair in front of the door, that was going to come across as majorly suspicious.

With her heart pounding, she went back to the place where she'd been headed when Mack had first come in—the closet, with the secret piece of equipment that wasn't in any of the other bedrooms.

In the woods, Danny Preston wanted to scream in frustration. After Bradley and Wardman had escaped from his show in the woods, he'd scratched around for a plan B.

Probably they'd warned everyone to stay away from the other side of the wall, so luring someone else out here was a long shot, which meant that his only option was getting in there.

With his lips set in a grim line, he conjured up an army of little men and lined them up, ready to assault the wall that separated him from the hotel grounds. He sent them alone and in groups rushing toward the wall. But each time they vanished as they hit the barrier.

"Fuck," he growled and slammed his fist against the trunk of the tree that he'd made his main base of operation. The bark dug into his hand, and he cursed again. The sensation was real enough, and he pressed his hand against his side, willing the pain to subside. He supposed that if the bark had been sharp, it would have cut his flesh. Unfortunately he was as vulnerable as any of the hotel guests. This place could hurt him, probably kill him if he did something stupid. Or maybe taking this assignment was as far as he could go into the realm of stupidity.

He clenched his teeth. He wasn't here because he'd decided to invade someone's private playground. He'd been hired to do a job, and he hadn't had much choice about taking it. He'd come this far, but partial success wasn't good enough. Which meant he'd better think of some trick to get in there, identify his target and finish the job. Or was there another way to get an entrée? Pulling out his cell phone again, he made a call to one of the people who was standing by to help him.

The phone was answered on the first ring.

"Not going so well?" his associate asked. It wasn't the guy who'd hired him but someone he could theoretically trust.

"You could say that. I'm going to need a little help." Quickly he began to outline what he had in mind.

"You want me to *what?*" the other man asked.

"Just do it. You know I'll make it worth your while."

"What if I get caught?"

"I'd advise against it," he answered and clicked off. It was satisfying to put someone else on the spot—but would it do him any good in the long run?

Mack looked up and down the hall, glad that he was alone as he turned back and listened at Lily's door. When he didn't hear anything, he got out the keycard again and shoved it into the lock. Once again, it opened the door, and he couldn't repress a little smile of satisfaction. Maybe the locks didn't work to keep anyone from locking himself in his room and going quietly nuts—like that first guy, Jay Douglas, had done not so quietly.

Once again, Mack hurried down the interior hall. Lily wasn't in the bedroom. She wasn't in the bathroom, but she'd been going into the closet when he'd come here earlier. Now he threw the door open and stared inside. Lily wasn't there, but he saw some kind of interior door, closing off an area about the size of an old-fashioned telephone booth.

There was a knob and a keypad. He pushed some numbers at random without expecting any results. This wasn't going to be like the keycards.

Too bad he didn't know her birthday or anything else that might give him a clue.

Christ, now what? As far as he could tell, he'd found a secret room that you got to through the closet. Was it a door into the real world? Or could she be somewhere else in her room? Grimly, he searched the suite, looking behind furniture and under the bed, but she was gone—vanished like that guy Jay Douglas.

A shiver traveled over Mack's skin.

Had Lily been a figment of his imagination? That couldn't be true, could it? For a moment, he contemplated that idea. Jesus, since the breakup of his marriage, she was the first woman he'd wanted more from than good sex. What if he'd made her up because he needed her—or someone like her?

That thought made his chest tighten, until he fought back to rationality. He wasn't the only one who had seen her. The others in the bar had interacted with her. Unless he was making that up, too. Which would involve a whole new level of insanity on his part.

To reassure himself, he strode to the bed and lifted the top sheet, pressing it to his face. The scent of lovemaking was indisputable. He and Lily had been here together not long ago. If she was an illusion, she was the most realistic illusion he'd ever heard of. But then, where the hell had she gone?

CHAPTER FOURTEEN

Lily lay for a moment in the specially designed bed. She could hardly believe she was back in the real world, not after everything that had happened.

Hamilton had told her the stage set called the Mirador Hotel would seem absolutely authentic. She hadn't quite believed him. She'd expected some kind of barrier between herself and the altered reality. Instead, she had been *there*, right in the middle of everything with all the other hotel guests, like it was the only world that existed. That had never changed during the whole experience, but the rules of the place had shifted in ways she hadn't expected. Things had started happening that were impossible. Or should be impossible, at least according to the laws of physics.

She gave herself a few moments to adjust to being back in her physical body, then reached up and pulled off the cap that held the electrodes to her head, trying to focus on the task rather than the out-of-kilter experience—or the appealing man she'd been with a few minutes before.

Lord, what a mess. She hadn't planned on being so attracted to Mack Bradley. For years she'd focused on her work and not her social life. Now she'd finally met a man who made her yearn for all the things she'd denied herself, and she couldn't have him.

She closed her eyes and clenched her hands and teeth, trying not to think about that.

97

She'd lied to Mack about a lot of things. She wasn't a nurse. She was a doctor, a neurocyberneticist, who had taken what had seemed like an exciting job—to give men and women in a coma a chance for a life in a virtual reality by connecting their brain functions to a highly sophisticated computer program. It might not be in this world, but Hamilton had told her they wouldn't know the difference

Unfortunately, a lot of things weren't working out the way Dr. Hamilton had told her they would, starting with Jay Douglas's psychotic break that had caused him to attack her in the hotel lobby.

Okay, she supposed some failures were inevitable when you were dealing with damaged brains, a delicate interface and highly specialized equipment. Apparently Douglas hadn't been able to take the stress of waking up in a totally unfamiliar environment. Had Hamilton not anticipated something like that—or didn't he care?

But the screwup with Douglas didn't explain the other stuff—like the sky changing with impossible speed and the fantasy creatures attacking her and Mack in the woods. Hamilton hadn't prepared her for any of that. Had he known, or was he going to be as shocked as she was to find out their virtual reality was ... what? Under attack? Out of control? But how? And why?

When she'd disconnected herself from the machinery that had made it possible for her to enter the virtual environment, she felt a strange sense of loss. She should be glad to be back in the twenty-first century US of A. Glad that she *could* get back here. Yet now reality had a hollow feel.

With one hand on the bed rail, she sat up cautiously. She'd only been in there for a few hours, and the bed had kept her from lying in one position for too long, but she'd better take it slow while she adjusted to her normal body functions.

Where was Hamilton? And what about Mack?

She turned her head, and her insides clenched as she surveyed the rows of beds, each with a sleeping patient. She knew which was Mack. She'd been drawn back to him again and again.

Now she turned away, unable to deal with the difference in the pale, still Mack Bradley who was here and the Mack Bradley who had made love with her.

She had to put that aside—and put aside her own mistake of getting involved with Mack. Right now, she had to find Hamilton and demand to know what he wasn't telling her.

Mack was still searching the bedroom when a noise in the suite's other room made him whirl. Against all odds was she back? Or had someone else come in?

Reaching the area set up like a living-dining room, he stopped short. A cute little girl was sitting at the table, dipping a spoon into a bowl and carrying the contents to her mouth. Her blond hair was caught up in two medium-length ponytails at the sides of her head, and she was wearing a tee shirt with a kitten on the front, jeans and tennis shoes.

She looked up when she saw him and smiled.

"Hi," she said.

When he was still scrabbling for words, she went on, "This is really good."

He managed to ask, "What is it?"

"Ice cream. I haven't had anything this good in ..." She stopped and took her bottom lip between her teeth. "In a long time," she finally said in a low voice. "Maybe I could get you some."

"No thanks," he answered, wondering where it had come from and where she was going to get more. And at the same time, he was remembering that he hadn't been particularly hungry since he'd woken up here.

She tipped his head to the side, studying him. "If you're looking for Lily, you won't find her."

"Why not?"

"She's back in the world."

He felt a shiver travel over his skin as she confirmed his worst fear. "What does that mean?" he demanded.

"I'm not supposed to say."

It was a struggle to keep from shouting. "She told you not to say?"

"No. The Preston told me. He says he made ... special arrangements to bring me here, but I'll have to leave if I say too much ..." Her voice trailed off.

Anger and frustration made him want to stride across the room, take her by the shoulders, and shake her. But the look of confusion in her eyes stopped him. She wasn't being coy. He was pretty sure she didn't know much more than he did.

He cleared his throat and asked the question that had been circling around in his mind like a top whizzing around on a wooden floor.

"Are you Lily's sister—Shelly?"

She tipped her head to the side, studying him. "Yes. How did you know? I mean, we never met did we?" The last part sounded doubtful, as though she wasn't entirely sure.

"She talked about you."

"Like what did she say?"

"She told me you were in an accident."

"Uh huh."

"Did you come here to talk to Lily?"

"Uh huh. The Preston said I should, you know. But I guess I was too late."

He crossed the room, pulled out a chair and sat down at the table. "The Preston—what is that?

She shrugged. "A guy—I guess. He needs to get out of the woods, but he's stuck."

Mack had met a man in the woods—along with a bunch of little warriors and some dangerous animals.

100

"What does he look like?"

"Ugly."

"Like how?"

"His head was bald, and he had ... pictures on his arms. She clasped her hands together. One was a nasty snake. And one was a skull."

"What else?"

"Big, heavy, black boots. Dirty jeans."

She was describing the guy Mack had seen standing on the tree branch. The Preston? Maybe that was his name.

"How do you know him?"

"I don't. He just came and talked to me. I think he's not very nice." She stopped, then went on quickly, "But he was nice to bring me here."

"Why did he do that?"

She squirmed in her chair. "I guess he thinks Lily will do something, if I ask her to."

"Why?"

"Because she feels bad about my ... accident."

Maybe she was telling the truth. Or maybe not. Or maybe she was giving him a child's interpretation of events. He was sure she didn't like being questioned.

Dipping her head, she scraped at the ice cream bowl and ate a few more bites.

Was she human? Or was she just a fantasy projection like the creatures in the woods? Only in the form of a little girl instead of monsters.

And for that matter, was Mack Bradley human? Or was he just a figment of someone else's imagination?

The question made the breath freeze in his chest, and he struggled not to gasp for air.

Could he trust *anything* in this place that was as reliable as a fun-house mirror?

His vision had turned inward, and he didn't realize the girl was halfway out of her chair until she bolted for the door of the hotel suite. She'd taken Mack by surprise, and he was steps behind her as she leaped into the hall like a forest animal desperate to escape a hunter. He stopped short when he got to the doorway. She wasn't anywhere in sight. Could she have run fast enough to round a corner? Not unless she'd sprouted jets on her tennis shoes. Of course that could have happened in this place where the rules of physics seemed to have no meaning. Or she could simply have vanished. Again, a tribute to this fantasy-land outpost where it was impossible to know what to expect.

CHAPTER FIFTEEN

The address of Hamilton Labs was on a narrow road in an isolated area of Montgomery County out past Gaithersburg. As Grant drove slowly by, he took a good look at the three-story building constructed of cement slabs with few windows. He also noted the chain-link fence topped by razor wire and the security cameras at various locations around the exterior of the building. Clearly, whoever ran this place didn't want surprise visitors.

He turned around in a small woods about a mile past the building and drove by again, noting the location of the exits and the distance of the fence to the building. There were only five cars in the lot, which probably meant there weren't many people inside at this hour.

After the recon, he stopped by a nearby home improvement warehouse that was still open. Using more of the cash he'd taken from the dead man at the Roosevelt Memorial, he bought a wire cutter and some other equipment before heading back to the lab.

Glad that it was fully dark, he used the wire cutters to snip through a section of fence, then ducked inside and waited for several minutes. When no floodlights came on and no siren sounded, followed by armed men charging in his direction, he bent low as he ran to the closest car. Again he waited before sprinting to another vehicle that was closer to the building. This time, to make sure he hadn't tripped a silent alarm, he waited for ten minutes with the vehicle blocking him from view while he got some of his supplies out of his knapsack.

He'd taken the thugs at the Roosevelt Memorial by surprise with his ploy of arriving early. He was betting his life he could throw them off-balance again.

Five minutes later, the car was on fire, sending smoke and flames into the air. He hurried away into the darkness, pretty sure that guys who shot one of their own men weren't going to call in the local fire department for an auto fire on their own turf.

As he'd anticipated, a squad of men came running out with fire extinguishers, some from the main entrance and some from a door at the side of the building.

"Christ, how did that happen?" someone shouted.

"Looks like a diversion," a hard voice answered. The man speaking was Jack Wilson, who had ordered one of his own operatives cut down.

"A diversion from whom?"

"I'm betting on the brother."

"How would he find this place?"

"I don't know. But we're not taking any chances. Greg and Martin, check the parking lot. Tim and Brad, check the building interior."

Grant listened, thinking that two guys would be spread pretty thin in there, and the sooner he got inside, the better. Staying in the shadows, he moved toward the side door and slipped inside, weapon in hand. A long hallway lined with offices led to the front of the building. Looking into a few, he saw that some of the rooms were totally empty and others had desks and chairs that could have just been delivered from a rental furniture company, making the first floor look like it was designed to function as a buffer zone between the exterior and the upper floors

At the end of the corridor, he could see a security guard glued to the window, watching the men outside dealing with the burning car. Cole snorted. So much for the guy's doing his job. Before reaching the front of the building, Grant stepped into a stairway and hurried up, stopping at the door to listen.

When he eased it open, he found himself in another hallway with offices. Moving quietly, he looked in a few doors. Up here some of the offices were clearly in use, with computers and papers on the desks and coffee cups sitting next to some of them.

Still, he encountered no one and climbed the stairs to the next level. At the end of the hall, he came to a large room where he saw a very strange sight.

The place was full of beds. He had a good view of the nearest ones and saw sleeping men and women hooked to machinery. The beds moved, shifting the sleepers from time to time so that they were never lying in one position for long.

A surge of excitement rippled through Grant. Could one of them be his brother? Before he could find out, he saw that there was someone here besides the sleepers, a man dressed like an orderly stood beside one of the beds, massaging the legs of a sleeping man. His back was to Grant who quickly crouched behind one of the beds. The guy stopped, made notations on an electronic notepad he carried, then went on to another patient.

Voices from down the hall alerted Grant that someone was approaching, and he slipped between two of the beds where he hoped he couldn't be seen from either direction.

A man and a woman walked in, talking intently.

The orderly turned. "Dr. Hamilton. Dr. Wardman."

"Carry on, Durant," the man said.

Grant took a quick look. The man was in his fifties, Grant judged, and dressed in dark slacks and a white shirt. She was a pretty young brunette, probably in her thirties, wearing an outfit that looked like a medical scrub suit. She seemed to be in an agitated state, and the man was apparently trying to calm her.

Judging from the name of the lab and the man's apparently superior status, Grant would guess he was Hamilton—the guy who'd given the facility his name—and she was Wardman. But he could be wrong.

"We were expecting you back earlier," the one he assumed was Hamilton said.

"I couldn't get away sooner."

"And we couldn't exactly break the neural connection if you were with any of them."

"Right."

"Why couldn't you leave?"

She hesitated. "We had talked about my slipping away after the initial adjustment period, but everybody was nervous. They decided to stick together in the bar, and there wasn't an opportunity to be alone." She dragged in a breath before saying. "From their reactions, I think there should have been an orientation session—so the subjects would know what was going on."

"I wanted to see how they'd react without that information."

"Badly," she answered, sounding like she was trying to rein in anger.

"How so?"

"They were worried, frightened and confused."

"Uh huh."

His answer made it sound like he wasn't going to give on that point. Changing the subject, she blurted, "And it wasn't anything like I expected."

"Nothing?" the man asked, his voice growing sharp.

"Well, some of it was what we talked about before I went in. The environment was totally detailed, perfectly realistic. Landon did a marvelous job with the setting." She hesitated.

"What?"

"Well, one of the patients noted that the outside temperature was the same as the inside, which wouldn't be true in India."

"Okay. What else?"

"They all noted the lack of hotel staff. Someone asked about the liquor in the bar. If they drank from a bottle, would it be replenished in the morning?"

"I honestly don't know. We'll have to ask Landon."

She went on in a rush. "And what happened to Jay Douglas?"

"How did it appear from your end?"

"I encountered him in the lobby. He was ..." she stopped and thought. "I'd have to say acting paranoid and hostile. He attacked me."

Hamilton winced. "But you were okay? No—physical—damage?"

"One of the patients knocked him out."

"Which one?"

"Mack Bradley."

When he heard his brother's name, Grant felt a hot flare like an electric shock inside his chest. She'd said Mack Bradley. His brother. Mack was here. But he was one of the patients? And what did it mean? The patients were lying in these beds, but Wardman had said Mack saved her from an attack. How could he do that if he was a sleeping patient here?

Grant was trying to puzzle that out, but the doctors were talking again—apparently about the guy who had gone nuts. And Grant had better listen for clues.

"His records showed that he was mentally stable before he went in. Apparently the environment was too much for him, and he flipped out—for want of a better way to put it."

"And now?" the woman pressed.

"We kept close check on everybody. He went absolutely flat on the Glasgow Coma Scale. We could tell something was wrong, and we pulled him out, but we couldn't save him."

"What was the terminal event?" she asked, her voice going high at the end of the sentence.

"A cerebral hemorrhage."

The woman answered with a sound of acknowledgment, then asked, "What about Ben Todd? About his sense of taste?"

"Apparently his taste center sustained damage. He seemed otherwise normal?"

"Yes. He was aggressive. What you'd expect from a lawyer."

"I want to talk about the anomalies in the environment. Like the clouds you mentioned?"

"Okay."

Grant raised his head enough to see her again. She looked like she had come into contact with something completely outside her experience. Something she feared and could not explain in rational terms. "And the things in the woods."

Hamilton kept his speculative gaze fixed on her as though he thought she might be suffering from some kind of mental problem.

Before she could say more, Grant heard a discreet electronic ping.

The man held up his hand for her to stop talking, then pulled a cell phone from a holster on his belt.

"Hamilton," he said, confirming Grant's assumption.

He listened for a moment, then said, "That was Wilson. There may be a security breach in the building. I have to go downstairs for a few minutes."

"Can't he take care of it?"

"He wants to talk to me in person." Hamilton turned to the orderly. "Come with me."

The two men hurried out of the room, leaving Grant alone with the sleepers and the woman.

She stared after the departing figures, then ran a shaky hand through her hair before starting toward one of the beds,

"Just a minute," Grant said, standing, the gun held down by his leg where she wouldn't see it yet.

The movement must have startled her, and she whirled, staring at him with a mixture of astonishment and hope.

"Mack? My God, Mack?"

CHAPTER SIXTEEN

"You said my brother saved you from an attack?" Grant said.

Her eyes never left him, but now it looked like she was considering her earlier reaction to him when she'd said, "You're not Mack?"

Slowly she took a step closer, staring at his face. "No, you don't have the scar on your chin."

"Yeah. I'm Mack's brother, Grant," he answered, punching out the words, "And I want to know what the hell is going on here? You reacted like you thought I was him. Where the hell is he?"

Her expression took on a look of confusion. "Don't you know? I mean, didn't you give permission for him to join the program?"

Grant fought a surge of anger and his own confusion. "Christ. What is this, some kind of shell game? What program? Mack was supposed to be dead. I went to the funeral home and opened his coffin, and there was a blank-faced dummy inside instead of him."

She drew in a quick breath, her eyes widening as she took that in. "But I thought ..."

"What?" he demanded.

"That the families had agreed."

Somehow he kept himself from shouting. In as normal a voice as he could manage, he said, "I've been trying to figure out what was going on since I opened that coffin. Is my brother alive or dead?"

He waited with his heart pounding, watching her face contort as she gestured toward one of the beds.

"He's there. I was just going to see him."

"You're Doctor Wardman?"

"Yes. Lily Wardman."

Grant followed her past several beds where men and women were lying with their eyes closed, hooked up to wires and tubes.

Mack was occupying the next bed. His skin was pale, and his eyes were closed. He looked like he was barely alive.

Grant struggled forward, feeling like his arms and legs were suddenly weighted down with lead.

"Mack?" He reached out and touched his brother, startled and at the same time reassured that his skin was warm.

When they'd been boys, they'd had a special bond between them, a kind of private communication. It was like they'd been able to speak to each other without speaking words.

They had lost the ability as their bodies had changed from boys' to men's. Now he reached out, calling to his brother, trying to get through to the unconscious man on the bed.

Mack? Can you hear me, Mack? I've been searching all over hell for you. I finally found you, in some kind of lab. Can you hear me, Mack?

His brother's lids fluttered, and his eyes opened, focusing on Grant. Beside him, Lily Wardman gasped.

"Mack?" she said.

His lips moved, but no sound came out.

She stepped forward, reaching for his hand, squeezing it. "Mack? Can you hear me?"

"Yes."

"Thank God."

He kept his gaze focused on her. "Where are we?"

"At the Hamilton Labs."

111

But Mack's eyes had already closed again.

Mack Bradley felt his vision blur. He reached for the wall, steadying himself against the solid, vertical surface. For a moment the hotel vanished, and he thought he saw another scene. Then it was gone.

He fought to ground himself, and finally his vision cleared. Lifting his head, he looking around. He was still in the hallway of the hotel. He would swear he'd seen his brother—just for a moment. And heard Grant calling him inside his mind—the way they'd done it when they were kids. After the ability had slipped away, they'd been frustrated by not being able to rely on a form of communication that they'd taken for granted. But they'd finally had to accept that it wasn't coming back

Just now Grant had said something to him—mind to mind. And he'd had the strong impression that Lily was with him, which was even more confusing. Or had he been talking to Lily and not Grant. That was even weirder.

He didn't know where Lily had gone. And he didn't know where his brother was, either.

"Grant?" he said aloud and also silently. "Grant, is that you?"

It was curious to be reaching out to his brother in the old way now—after all this time. But if it was going to happen anywhere, why not in this place where the laws of physics had no meaning?

He felt a buzzing in his brain, like Grant was still trying to speak to him. But it was only a buzz, as though the power of that first jolt had dissipated.

He was left with the confusion of trying to sift through who had spoken to him. Grant or Lily? Could they be together somehow? Both trying to talk to him.

He spoke aloud, calling out to his brother, then Lily, alternating their names.

But neither of them answered, and Mack sensed there was no point in continuing to try and reach them again. At least not now.

For a moment Grant thought he'd gotten through to the man lying in the bed. Then the connection disappeared like a fantasy he'd conjured in his own brain. Fighting a deep sense of defeat, Grant looked up to see the woman staring at him with an expression that wavered between compassion and something he couldn't quite read. But perhaps her reaction was similar to his.

"I think he heard us," she whispered. "He ... he spoke."

"Yeah."

"I've tried to get through to him before, but he never said anything back. This time was different." She tipped her head to the side and looked at him. "He responded to you first."

"As you noticed, we're twins. We could speak to each other in our minds when we were boys. Then it ... went away. We hadn't done it in years—until now." He gave her a defiant look. "I'm not making it up."

"I know. I saw him open his eyes. I heard him say something," she said, like she was trying to remember the details of a dream.

Grant looked toward her, feeling his gaze sharpen as he fought to keep his balance in a world that had suddenly tilted to the side. "Wait a minute. You thought I was him when you first saw me. Walking around—not lying in this bed. Did you meet him when he was okay? I mean, what's going on?"

She dragged in a breath and let it out. "Not here. Well, I think he was responding to me here because I spent a lot of time with him. But I went into the virtual reality with him and the other people you see here." She stretched out her arm, indicating the people in the other beds.

Grant's eyes narrowed. "How about speaking English. Virtual reality? Maybe you'd better back up a couple of steps."

"Right. You don't really know about the program," she acknowledged, then seemed to be gathering her thoughts. "Okay, this lab was designed to give people with severe brain injuries— another chance at life."

"You have a way to wake them up?" he asked. "Like was that what just happened with Mack?"

"I'm sure he's going to wake up, but not the ones who suffered catastrophic brain injuries." She swept her arm toward the sleeping men and women. "All of these people, including Mack, are in a coma here, but at the same time, they can be in a virtual world where they can have something close to a normal existence."

He listened to her voice catch on the word "normal."

"You're lying."

"No. It was supposed to be pretty much like this world. Well, somewhere different. A nice place where they could relax. A luxury hotel."

He still wasn't quite getting it. Or maybe he didn't want to. "A place to relax? What are you talking about?"

She turned one hand up. "As far as they're concerned, they're at a hotel in a lush foreign setting so they wouldn't be focused on what was happening back home. That was the theory." She made a low sound. "But when they woke up, they were all worried about where they were. We should have thought about that," she added, as though making a mental note.

"You mean they woke up in a strange place and were trying to figure out why?"

"Yes."

"How do you know?"

"I was in there with them. That's where I was talking to Mack," she answered softly.

The gentle way she said it, made him study her carefully. "Talking?"

She flushed and looked away, then started speaking rapidly. "But something happened in there that we didn't plan. Some outside force has gotten in. That's the only way I can explain it."

"Uh huh." The whole thing was beyond weird, especially the last part, but he wanted to know what was going on with his brother. "And what are you saying about Mack, exactly?"

He saw her swallow. "I told Dr. Hamilton he shouldn't be part of the experiment. His neck got twisted when he had to bail out of his fighter jet. His lower brain functions were compromised, but they seem to be coming back. I mean, we both saw him wake up—briefly."

"And that means he's going to wake up and get out of that bed?"

"We don't know yet. There's no way to predict his recovery in this kind of situation."

Grant nodded, knowing she was doing the medical tango—dancing around predictions when you didn't know what was going to happen. Still, he was about to press for more information when a sharp voice interrupted the private exchange.

"What is going on here?"

The question came from the man who had left the room earlier—Dr. Hamilton. He stared at Grant.

"Bradley?"

"Yeah."

"But that's impossible."

When he reached for his phone, Grant raised the gun he'd been holding and at the same time grabbed Dr. Wardman and pulled her back against his chest.

She gasped and tried to wrench herself away.

"Stay still and you won't get hurt," he said, punching out the words.

When his captive quieted, he looked at Dr. Hamilton.

"Put your phone away, and don't come any closer to me," he ordered. "You're going to tell me how I can get my brother out of here and back to a normal life."

CHAPTER SEVENTEEN

Grant noted the look of panic that flashed across the doctor's features. Was he worried about his colleague getting hurt or that Grant was going to screw up his experiment?

As though he had settled on how he should be reacting, he said, "Don't hurt her."

"I won't, if you cooperate," Grant answered in a hard voice, acting like he was a two-bit thug who'd broken into this place to steal drugs or something. "Tell me what's going on here," he said, asking the same question that he'd asked the woman and wondering if he was going to get the same answer.

"Wait—you're Mack Bradley's brother?"

"Yes."

"Your brother is in a very new program."

"That you were supposed to get permission to put him in," Grant spat out.

The doctor blanched. "I thought we had permission."

"I think you're lying about that little detail."

Instead of denying it, the doctor challenged, "What do you want me to do about it?"

"Get him out of here."

"I'm sorry. That's impossible. If he leaves this lab, he'll die."

While Grant coped with that, the doctor kept speaking.

117

"But your brother is lucky to be here. We call this the Phoenix Project. We're saving people who are the victims of traumatic brain injury."

Grant looked toward the beds of sleeping patients. "They all look like they're the next thing to dead," he answered, wincing when he thought of how that applied to his brother.

"No, we've created a place where they can live. A virtual reality."

Wardman had told him that, and he hadn't really wrapped his mind around the concept.

"Which means?"

"They are living normal lives—in a controlled environment. A place where they can feel healthy and productive." He became more enthusiastic as he continued. "Like what if people who had been in car wrecks or been shot or had heart attacks could be kept alive and functioning in another reality?" Now the doctor sounded like he was making a funding pitch. "You've heard of Seymour Cray, right? The genius behind high performance computers who died after an automobile accident."

Grant had some vague memory of the man and nodded. He'd certainly heard of the Cray Computer.

"What if he'd had a place to keep working designing computers instead of having to go off life support because the doctors thought his case was hopeless? Multiply his circumstances by hundreds."

"And what about my brother? I was told he was dead, but there was a dummy in his casket. If he wasn't stolen for this project, then what's going on?"

"All I know is that he was registered as a legitimate subject," Hamilton denied, but his sick look told Grant that he was either outright lying or suspected that there had been something funny about Mack's participation.

Lily cleared her throat.

"What?" Mack snapped.

"I'm not going anywhere. Would you turn me loose and put the gun down?"

When he loosened his hold on her, she moved quickly away, then turned to face him and Hamilton. She fixed her gaze on the other man.

"The project's not exactly going the way we expected. I mean like Jay Douglas having a total mental breakdown."

Hamilton's voice rose. "Do not talk about any of that in front of an outsider."

She looked like there was a lot more she wanted to say, but when she glanced at Grant, she fell silent.

He let his gaze travel from one to the other of them. They both looked upset, but he had the feeling that their concerns were somewhat different. He'd bet Lily cared about the people in there—and Hamilton cared about his research.

"Is there any way to contact my brother and find out what's going on in there," Grant asked, thinking that he needed something more reliable than the ability they'd shared when they were kids.

Hamilton looked relieved that the focus of the conversation had shifted somewhat. "We can ask Sidney Landon."

"Who's that?"

"Our programmer. He designed the whole setup."

"Okay. Get him," Grant ordered.

Hamilton walked to the desk along one wall and picked up the phone.

Grant stayed beside him. "No funny stuff. Put it on speaker."

"Yes." The doctor pressed the speaker button, then punched in a number. When a man answered, he said,

"Can you come down to the lab?" he said.

They heard an agitated voice say, "I'm kind of busy up here."

"Because?" Hamilton asked, his tone sharp.

119

"I spent a lot of time designing that VR and making the system secure. But it looks like someone has hacked into it. I'm trying to figure out who it is and what the hell they're doing."

Lily gasped. Hamilton's face had turned ashen.

"You said it was impregnable," the older man bellowed.

"I thought it was. It should have been, for God's sake. But it looks like someone went to a lot of trouble to get past the barriers I set up. You know, similar to the crap that's been going on with companies like Sony and Target. Someone made a concerted effort to get in *there.* But they're public companies. Who would know about the Phoenix Project?"

"I don't know." The doctor's face hardened as he went on the attack. "I'm paying you good money for a quality product."

"It *is* a quality product."

Grant interrupted the angry exchange.

"Is there any way to communicate with the people in there? They may be able to help figure out what's going on—or give you some clues."

"Who's speaking?" Landon asked.

"This is Grant Bradley, the brother of one of the patients."

"Mack Bradley?"

"Yeah. How can I get in touch with him?"

"I ..."

Dr. Wardman jumped into the conversation. "Mack and I both had some extensive contact with the hacker."

"Jesus. How?" Landon asked, his voice wavering between upset and hopeful.

"We saw him in the woods on the other side of the wall at the back of the hotel. He came up with a fantasy show for us."

"Like what?"

"Weird vegetation. Weird animals. Warlike little men." Mack can tell you more about it."

"Okay," Landon said. "I'll be right down."

120

The connection snapped off, and the three people awake in the lab looked at each other.

"Why would someone hack into your virtual reality?" Grant asked Hamilton.

The researcher shook his head. "I have no idea. I mean, who even knows about it?" he asked Landon's question again.

The way he said the last part made Grant's skin tingle.

"I think you have an idea who knows about it," he answered keeping his gaze on the doctor. It was tempting to raise his gun again and point it at the man, but he managed not to make a threatening move.

Hamilton looked torn but finally said, "My backer. But why would he get someone to hack in?"

"To check up on you."

Hamilton had turned pale.

Before Grant could back the guy into a corner, a wiry young man burst into the lab. His collar-length hair looked like he'd been running his fingers through it every few seconds for the past few hours. His blue work shirt and plaid slacks looked like he'd been wearing them for weeks. And his face had the pasty color of someone who'd been living in a cave for months. Too bad you couldn't get a healthy tan from a computer screen.

Grant wanted to ask Hamilton where he'd gotten this guy, but that would have to wait until later. And really, from his appearance, it looked like he was a genuine programing geek.

"You can put me in touch with my brother?" he asked.

The man glanced at the chief researcher. "I thought we agreed there would be no contact with the outside world until they acclimate."

"We may not have that luxury," Hamilton answered. "Not if someone from outside is screwing with the system."

"Yeah, okay," Landon muttered. "He looked at Grant. "I have a way to get in there that will seem fairly normal to the people in the hotel. I don't know if he'll get the message."

"He'd better," Grant warned, wondering what he was going to do if the guy's plan didn't work.

Landon settled himself in front of a computer terminal at the side of the room and started typing. Grant paced back and forth as he watched the man typing on the keyboard.

Mack had just come down to the lobby to find out what was going on among the other hotel guests when he heard people calling his name.

"Something wrong?" he asked.

"Where were you?" Paula Rendell asked.

"In my room." Not exactly accurate, but he wasn't going to say he'd been in Lily's suite making love with her. And then she'd vanished. He imagined how the others would *react to that.*

Paula's eyes narrowed. "Maybe we should have everybody's room number, since there's no good way to get in touch with each other."

"About what?"

"Well, you might want to know that your name is flashing on the computer screens in the business center."

"Jesus." He'd been trying to act laid back. Now he dashed across the lobby and into the center, where he saw that the words "Mack Bradley" were indeed flashing in red on the three screens.

He went to one of the computers and looked at the setup, frustration and excitement warring inside him. Finally he saw an instant message icon and pressed it. When a chat box popped up, he typed a question mark.

"Mack?" The answer came back immediately.

"Who is this?" he asked.

"Grant."

He hadn't known what he was expecting. Maybe he'd been secretly fearing something like what had happened in the woods. Certainly not a communication from his brother.

"Is that really you?" he asked cautiously. This could still be some kind of scam.

"Yes."

"Prove it."

"You were the captain of the football squad when Cumberland won the championship," the person on the other end of the line typed back.

"Anyone could look that up." Mack looked back at Paula. "Maybe you'd better give me some privacy."

When she didn't move, he propelled her out the door and closed it before turning back to the screen.

A new message said, "Okay. We used to send each other silent messages. Nobody knows about that. And a little while ago, I called out to you—and I'm pretty sure you answered."

He felt a chill travel over his skin. Yes, he thought he had heard Grant, calling him from some place outside this setup. "My God, how did you find me?"

"Long story." There was a pause, and Grant came back. "Are you alone?"

"Yes."

"They said I can switch to a video hookup."

Mack waited with his heart pounding, still unable to quite believe that this was really happening.

When his brother's face appeared on the screen, Mack felt a wave of relief so profound that he fought not to choke up. He'd been wondering where he was and sure it wasn't the real world. Now Grant was going to tell him the truth.

He stared at his twin, seeing from his expression that his reaction was as emotional as Mack's. What did that mean?

"Hey," he managed to say.

"Back at ya," Grant answered.

"Where are you?" Mack clenched his fists, then struggled to relax. "Well, maybe more important—where am I?"

When he saw Grant swallow hard, he was pretty sure he wasn't going to like the answers. "I'm at a facility called Hamilton Labs. To give you the executive summary, you were supposed to be dead. I got here after finding a dummy in your coffin."

Mack's shocked curse ran through the business center and apparently into the lobby. When someone—probably Paula—pounded on the door, he shouted, "Later."

"Are you all right?" she yelled back.

"Yeah. I'll get back to you in a while."

"What was that?" Grant asked.

"I'm in the business center. The others are wondering what's up. So why don't you explain what the hell is going on before they break down the door," he pressed. "Where is this place?"

Grant waited a beat before answering. "You're in a virtual reality. Do you know what that means?"

After taking a moment to process the answer, he asked uncertainly, "Like in a video game?"

"Something like that. I was told you'd died in ... well in whatever country where you were flying missions." His brother gave him a quick account of the missing body in the coffin and Grant's demands for information.

"You and the other people in there are part of an experiment," Grant added.

"Like how?"

His brother swallowed hard before answering. "The good news is that it's a place where you can function. The bad news is that everyone there is in a coma back here at the lab."

"Jesus! You're kidding."

"No. Your neck was twisted when you ejected. It caused ... damage."

Mack tried to absorb that information and found that he'd been preparing for bad news since he arrived here. "Am I going to get better?" he managed to ask.

"There's a good chance you can recover," his brother said. "Remember, I said I called to you. And you opened your eyes and looked at me—and spoke."

"When?"

"A few minutes ago. Did you hear me?"

"Yeah."

Grant glanced over his shoulder, and another person entered the screen. When Mack saw it was Lily, his heart stopped, then started to pound.

"I see you're back home," he said in a bitter voice. "What about the coma part?"

"I'm not one of the patients," she whispered.

"You're some kind of spy?"

Her hand flattened against her chest as if she were trying to repress the beating of her own heart. "I'm one of the researchers."

She looked entirely miserable, but he couldn't let himself be swayed by what she might be regretting now. The bottom line was that she'd lied to him in a lot of different ways—starting when he'd rescued her from that Jay Douglas guy. Probably she'd know what was wrong with Douglas.

"And your role?" he asked in a sharp voice. "You were sent to keep an eye on us?"

"Well, to help you adjust," she whispered, and he saw moisture glittering in her eyes.

He snorted, determined not to let this get personal—again. "You weren't doing such a great job."

"We both know stuff started happening that wasn't ... expected."

"Are you really a nurse?"

"I'm a doctor."

"Figures," he muttered, hoping his own face didn't reveal his bitter disappointment. Finally, he'd connected with a woman on a more than physical level, only it had all been a charade on her part.

He wanted to ask what making love with him had meant to her. But not in front of his brother and whoever else was there. And why waste the time talking about something that had become completely irrelevant?

Behind her, a gruff voice said, "We set up this connection so you could help us figure out who hacked into the system. Do you have any useful information?"

CHAPTER EIGHTEEN

Two more people crowded into the picture, an older man and a guy who looked like Central Casting had sent him to play the part of a computer nerd.

Mack ignored the others and focused on Lily, seeing the way her eyes still watered. That was almost enough to get to him—but not quite. Not after the way she'd pulled a couple of very slick cons on him. She'd pretended to be one of the gang. Then she'd pretended she cared about him.

The last observation made him feel like he was looking at her through a jagged broken window, and if he reached for her, he was going to slash his skin.

He wasn't going to make the mistake of trusting her again, but he kept his gaze on her because he needed to see her reaction to what he was about to say.

"After you left, something really weird happened. Your sister came to your room."

She blinked, probably startled by the abrupt change of subject—and the topic itself.

"What are you talking about?"

"About the little girl who came looking for you. She was eating ice cream, and she said it was the best thing she'd tasted in years."

"My God. My sister. That's impossible."

"She said she was Shelly."

"What did she look like?" Lily asked in a barely audible voice.

"Cute," he answered, giving his overall impression first. "Her hair was blond and done up in a couple of ponytails, one on each side of her head, and she was wearing a tee shirt with a kitten on the front. She had kind of scruffy jeans and tennis shoes."

Lily caught her breath. "That … that's what she was wearing when she was in the auto accident. But how could she be there? She's in a hospital in Virginia."

"Your sister?" an older man repeated.

She looked back at him. "Yes. I told you about her. She's in a nursing facility in Fairfax."

"Oh—right. But … how could she get into our setup?"

"Someone would have to hack her in," the computer nerd answered.

"How is that possible?" the older man asked.

"I don't know."

"Who are you?" Mack interrupted, addressing the older guy.

The man gave him a direct look. "Philip Hamilton. I'm the principal investigator here."

"Oh, nice to meet you," Mack said, putting as much sarcasm as he could manage into the greeting. "You mean you're responsible for this mess?" he added, in case the principal researcher didn't get his response.

"It's not a mess. We're doing good work—for you and the others."

"Maybe that was your intention, but something else has overtaken you."

Lily stepped closer to the screen, blocking Mack's view of Hamilton. "You were saying that my sister is there."

"She was. She … vanished."

He could see she was fighting disappointment.

"Did she say how she got there?"

"Yes. That's the important point. She said the Preston in the woods brought her."

"The Preston—what the hell is that?" Hamilton called out from in back of Lily.

"A man in the woods. She said his head was bald, and he had ... pictures on his arms. He's the guy Lily and I saw in there."

"It must be the hacker," the computer nerd muttered. "He put himself physically into the VR."

"And who are you?" Mack asked.

"Sidney Landon, the designer."

"And putting us in a hotel in India was your clever idea?"

"I was there last year. I liked it. It's the most luxurious place I've ever visited," the guy said defensively. "And they have a really good Web site with a virtual tour of the interior and exterior. That made my work a lot easier."

Mack snorted. "Nice for you."

"What about the hacker?" Landon asked. "You said you saw him in there?"

"I saw him—but not in the hotel. He's in the woods outside the grounds. I don't think he can actually get in here."

"Why not?" Landon asked.

"Because I'm pretty sure he wants to. The best he can do is create weird effects in the clouds and in the woods." When Mack described the strange clouds and recounted some of what happened in the woods, the designer whistled.

"He's talented," Landon muttered. "Too talented. But at least some of my protections are holding." He tipped his head to the side as he looked at Mack. "Do you think the girl was who she said she was? Or did he create her?"

Mack considered the answer. "I don't think he created her. First, if he'd made her, he'd need to have a lot of information to do it right. She was expecting to talk to Lily, not me. And Lily could ask her questions, just the way I quizzed Grant before I believed it was really him. Second, I don't think she would have talked about him if he'd created her."

"Fair points."

"And the next question is—why is he trying to invade your video game? For the challenge of getting in? Or does he want something specific? Or someone?" Mack added.

"We need to find out," Landon answered.

Lily, who had been absent for several minutes, crowded into the group around the computer screen again. "I called the facility where my sister is being cared for. She's still there."

"You said the accident was years ago," Mack said. "What about her body? I mean, she can't still be a little girl, can she?"

"No. Her body has grown up."

"Not in the VR. I guess that's how she still thinks of herself."

Lily's eyes widened. "You mean, she could have some kind of life—inside her mind—inside the VR."

Mack caught the hope in her voice and answered softly, "I think so."

Hamilton jumped back into the conversation, a triumphant note in his voice. "That proves my point. The VR is functioning the way it's supposed to. She was there, and she was enjoying her ice cream. Didn't she say it was the best thing she had tasted in years? Maybe she should be brought here and hooked into the project."

Mack focused on the look of repressed joy on Lily's face, thinking the guy was clever. If he offered her hope for her sister, maybe she'd give him what he wanted.

In the real world, Mack saw Hamilton slip into the background and pull a mobile phone out of his pocket and make a call. A moment ago he'd looked elated. Now he looked worried.

Mack made eye contact with Lily, then shifted his gaze toward Hamilton. She gave a little nod and edged toward the doctor, who was talking in a low voice.

. . .

Grant was watching the byplay between the two doctors, Mack and the VR designer when the orderly who had been in the room earlier burst through the door and addressed Hamilton.

"Doc, those guys downstairs are doing a very thorough search of the first floor. When they finish, they'll be on their way up here."

Hamilton's head jerked up, and he said something to whoever was on the other end of the line. Apparently he didn't like the answer he'd gotten.

Grant strode toward the doctor. "He's talking about the men who tried to kill me at the Roosevelt Memorial. They're the reason I found this place."

"What?" Hamilton gasped. "Someone tried to kill you?"

"That wasn't your idea?" Grant shot back

The doctor's wide-eyed expression told Grant that he hadn't hatched the murder plan.

"And if they find me here, they're going to finish the job," Grant said. "Is there another way out?"

CHAPTER NINETEEN

Hamilton looked wildly around the room like he had just gotten there and didn't know the lay of the land.

It was Lily who answered. "The only other exit leads into the hall. Can we hold them off some way?" she asked, her voice rising in panic.

"They seem pretty goal oriented," Grant answered. "Do you have weapons up here? I mean besides my gun."

"I don't think so." She looked toward Hamilton. "What are we going to do?"

The doctor must have been already thinking about the problem. "We can hide him in the VR, using Jay Douglas's bed. They won't know he died."

Her expression was doubtful. "With no physical exam and no preparation?"

"How safe is it?" Grant asked.

"I wouldn't ... advise it," she answered. "We haven't done any tests on you to make sure you're compatible."

Hamilton was speaking to Durant, the orderly. "If they come up here, try to buy us a few minutes. Tell them we're having a crisis with one of the patients and we need to focus on stabilizing him."

Grant looked at his brother's image on the TV screen, then turned back to Hamilton. "Let's do it. I think I'm in better health than your average patient."

"You're coming in here?" Mack shouted from the terminal.

"Yeah," Grant answered. "It's the only place I can hide."

Lily made a strangled sound, then snapped into medical mode. "Take off your clothes."

He began shedding clothing as she crossed to a cabinet and pulled out one of the gowns the other patients were wearing.

"Put this on."

Already shirtless, Grant pulled his arms through the sleeves of the gown. Then he took off his pants.

Lily swept up his clothing and stuffed it into the bottom of a laundry basket.

It was all happening so fast that Grant hardly had time to decide if he'd made a fatal mistake by agreeing to this.

Hamilton had also swung into action, issuing orders as he ushered Grant to the bed.

"Lie down," he said to Grant, then to Landon, "And turn off the hookup to the VR. I don't want them to think we're in communication with anyone there."

"In a minute," Lily said, then spoke to Landon. "If he's going in there, I want him to arrive in the business center where Mack will be waiting for him."

"On the couch?" Landon asked.

"Yes," Hamilton answered. He turned back to Grant who was already lying on the bed.

"And we should start the process but not send him in until we're sure everything's okay," Lily added.

Hamilton gave her a look that said he didn't like taking orders from his second in command, but he continued working.

Lily kept her focus on Grant as she attached an IV line to his arm with impressive speed and efficiency then pulled a heavy plastic cap with electrodes down on his head.

Hamilton had a hypodermic in his hand, which he jammed into Grant's other arm and said, "Count backwards from one hundred."

He got as far as ninety-seven before the world around him faded out of existence.

. . .

The breath froze in Lily's lungs as the door to the lab burst open and three hard-faced men stepped in, all of them with handguns raised. They looked like they were ready to shoot first and ask questions later. She hadn't quite believed Grant when he'd said they'd tried to kill him. Now she understood how dangerous they were.

She wanted to look away, but it was impossible not to keep her gaze on them.

Were they going to start mowing everyone down? From the corner of her eye, she watched Hamilton straighten and turn to face the intruders.

"You can't simply burst into the laboratory."

"We didn't find the guy we were looking for downstairs. Where is he?"

The orderly, who was behind the intruders, gave the researchers a panicked look. Lily was thankful that they couldn't see his face.

Hamilton shook his head. "I have no idea. We haven't seen anyone who's not supposed to be in the building. And you have no call to hold us at gunpoint."

"Not if you're being straight with us. Mind if we have a look around?"

Hamilton swept his hand to the side, "Be my guest."

"All of you, over there," the man ordered.

The staff huddled together in the corner while the men moved around the patient area, looking under beds and glancing at the patients.

Lily's heart was pounding so hard that she thought it might crash through the wall of her chest. Her breath froze in her lungs as the searchers walked between the beds, looking under each, ignoring the patients.

When the three men finished in the room, the leader turned to Hamilton.

"I hope for your sake you're not lying to us."

"Why would I?"

"To double cross Mr. Sterling."

Lily heard genuine outrage in Hamilton's voice. "That's ridiculous. He and I have a good working relationship."

"Let's hope so."

The doctor had put on a good show of bravado. But as soon as the search team had disappeared into the elevator, he pulled out one of the desk chairs and sat down heavily.

"Are you okay?" Lily asked, taking in his paper-white skin.

"Yes."

She looked toward the bed where Grant was lying. "Thank God they didn't find him."

"Did you finish hooking him up?"

"I hope so."

"You don't know?"

She shook her head.

Hamilton heaved himself up, walked back to the new patient, and checked the monitor. "So far, he's stable."

So far. Great.

She looked toward Landon. "Don't send him in yet."

"Fine."

Swinging back toward Hamilton, she watched him fiddle with the equipment, thinking that he was doing it to keep from looking at her. "Those men work for Avery Sterling, the man who came in with money when you needed it to keep the project going?"

"Yes."

"You knew he had thugs on his payroll?"

"They're not thugs. They're his private security force."

She made a scoffing sound. "Who hold their employer's associates at gunpoint?'

"I never saw them in action."

"Why does he need guys like that working for him?"

"He's rich. I assume he has enemies."

She recalled the way Sterling had come into the building a few months ago and taken over Hamilton's office like he owned the place.

"And you investigated him before taking the money?"

He looked down at his hands. "Somewhat."

She wanted to scream that "somewhat" wasn't good enough. But she remembered her boss's panic when expected government funding hadn't come through, and he'd thought they were going to have to give up on the program. And to be honest, she remembered her own panic. They'd already accepted half their patients. What would have happened to those poor people if the project had been canceled before it started?

Still she was shocked at how things were shaking out—starting with Grant's revelation that he hadn't given permission for his brother to be part of the experiment. And then the information that someone had tried to kill him to keep him quiet—presumably these same men.

"What do you actually know about Sterling?" she asked.

"He's a respectable business man. He has a company that produces industrial chemicals that sell all over the world."

"That's all?"

"I know he gives generously to charities. He asked about the program and was excited by our work. He offered to provide us with funding."

Lily kept the questions coming. "What's his motivation for getting involved with the Phoenix Project?"

"He said he had a relative who had been in a car crash and ended up in a coma. He was desperate to give him a new life and wanted him in the program. He did some research, learned about the early papers I'd written, and decided to see what I was doing now."

"And after that he sends a hit squad after a man who was trying to find out what had happened to his brother?" she challenged.

"We don't know that was Sterling's men. And perhaps Bradley was mistaken about their intentions."

"They looked like they were prepared to wipe us out," she said.

"They wouldn't."

"How do you know?"

He gave her a smug look that she would have ignored when she was excited about joining his program. Now it made her insides clench. "Because if we're dead, there's no one to keep his relative alive."

"Okay," she said, understanding that logic and understanding that he had no doubt about who had sent the gunmen. "Which one of the patients is his relative?"

"That's confidential."

"Is it a man or woman?"

"Like I said, confidential."

She thought over the people she'd met in the VR. No one seemed more likely than any of the others. Well, she silently amended, it wasn't Mack Bradley.

"And how did Sterling find out about the project?" she asked, switching her thoughts back to the man who had seen his goon squad in here looking for Grant.

"As I said, he researched me."

She threw out another question she would have asked before taking Sterling's money. "Did he tell you the project had to stay secret?"

Hamilton swallowed. "For the time being."

She nodded. She had a lot more questions, but there was no time to press Dr. Hamilton now. In the past hour, he'd gone down a lot of notches in her estimation, but she couldn't simply walk away from him—not when Grant was hooked up to the equipment and about to go into the VR. And not when Mack and the others were in there and at the mercy of the Phoenix Project.

"And trying to kill the brother of one of the patients is a legitimate way to keep our project confidential?"

"No." The researcher looked toward the door, then looked at the other people who'd just been held at gunpoint. "I had no idea he would order tactics like that. If it was him."

"If it's him, what are we going to do?" she challenged.

"It goes without saying that we're all staying here until this thing is resolved." He looked at each of them in turn. Everyone nodded, but Lily wondered if Durant was going to bail out, since he had the least investment here.

Maybe Hamilton was thinking the same thing because he said to the orderly, "And I'll be paying you double your hourly wage."

"Yes, sir. Thanks."

"The phone call you got while we were talking to Mack was from Sterling?" she asked.

He hesitated for a moment, then said, "Yes."

"Maybe you'd better tell him we need a safe working environment."

"Right."

She clenched and unclenched her hands, wondering if she was making a foolish decision. "But before you do, I want to go back into the VR."

She wasn't sure if Hamilton would put up objections, but his quick agreement unsettled her. Did he think that sending her into the VR was a good way to get rid of her?

She glanced toward Landon, who looked like he was going to throw up whatever it was he'd had for lunch. She knew from office conversations with him that he'd seen the Phoenix Project as an exciting challenge, a chance to take Virtual Reality into a whole new realm.

"Is it stable in there?" she asked.

"At the moment, yes."

"Keep trying to get rid of the hacker."

"Of course," he bit out.

"My sister said his name was Preston. Does that mean anything to you?"

He shook his head.

"Maybe you can get a line on him—find out something that might be useful."

"Yeah."

"Keep the computer hookup open in the business center so we can talk if we have to."

"Okay."

She thought for a moment. "And can you have me return directly there instead of to my room?"

"I'd have to fiddle with some stuff."

"Why can you send Grant there?"

"He's a new subject. I set up his entry point there. Yours is in your bedroom."

"Okay. Wait a couple of minutes, and send him in. As soon as I arrive, I'll head downstairs."

"Yeah. You might need some stuff from your room."

"Uh huh," she answered, wondering if Grant was going to need medical attention.

She went to the storage cabinet where the gowns were kept and took one out. As Grant had done, she pulled the top on, then shucked out of her slacks. When she was dressed like one of the patients, she lay down in the bed she'd occupied before.

Hamilton came over and began attaching the necessary equipment. Like Grant, she wasn't in a coma, which meant she needed to be sedated.

She'd been excited when Hamilton had initially suggested sending her into the environment Landon had created. Now she couldn't shake a feeling of dread. There were too many ways to die in there—but she wasn't going to leave Mack and Grant to face them alone, starting with her conviction that Grant might not survive the transition without help.

She hung on to that conviction as Hamilton got her ready to leave reality. She didn't know what she was going to find when she went back to the Mirador Hotel—either on a professional level or a personal one.

Probably Mack would never trust her again, and that conclusion made her insides knot. But she cared about him, and she knew he and his brother might need her in that dangerous and unpredictable environment.

CHAPTER TWENTY

A gagging sound behind Mack made him whirl. His eyes bugged out when he saw a man wearing the standard hotel running outfit lying on the couch, his body jerking. The man's face was red and scrunched up as he coughed.

It was his brother.

"Grant," Mack shouted as he crossed the room in a few quick strides. His twin seemed to be choking.

When he continued to jerk and cough, Mack sat him up, leaning his twitching body against his own arm and pounded on his back—which had no effect. He remembered about the Heimlich maneuver, of course, but that was for people who were eating and had gotten something stuck in their throat. He didn't think that applied to Grant. He must be having some kind of reaction, maybe because sending him here had been done in a tearing hurry.

Grant's body shook in his arms, then suddenly went limp. Mack eased him to his back. He'd stopped coughing, but his skin had turned pale.

Mack stretched out his mind—trying to connect with Grant the way they had when they were boys, the way they had a couple of hours ago. But he couldn't feel his brother's thoughts, and that sent a new wave of panic through him.

"Grant," he whispered. "Don't leave me now, Grant."

A pounding on the door made his head jerk up. "Let me in."

It was Lily, also dressed in the standard running suit.

141

He ran to the door and unlocked it, seeing the crowd of people gathered in the lobby, their wide-eyed attention on the business center.

"What?" George Roper called out.

Before he could say more, Lily closed the door behind her. She was carrying a medical bag which she set on the table and opened. He saw standard stuff inside, like gauze and bandages, and other things that looked less like first-aid equipment.

She bent over Grant, holding his face in her hands, then pressing her palm to his chest.

"What's wrong?" Mack gasped.

"Difficult transition. Ideally he should have had more prep time."

She pulled out a hypodermic, loaded it from a vial, and squirted some liquid from the end before turning over Grant's arm, slapping her hand against the inside of his elbow and finding a vein. She stuck in the needle and depressed the plunger. Then she stepped back, letting Mack get closer.

The breath froze in his lungs as he stared at his brother, praying that he was going to respond. Glacial eons dragged by before he saw a flicker of Grant's eyelids. Then his eyes blinked open, and he looked around as though he couldn't quite believe where he was.

He focused on Mack.

"You made it. Thank God."

"Looks like it." Grant pushed himself up.

Mack reached for him, and they embraced.

"I thought you were dead," Grant whispered.

"I thought you were gonna be."

"But we're both here," Mack managed to say around the lump in his throat. He thought he'd never see his brother again, or anyone else he knew. Now here they were together. Too bad it was in this hellhole outside the known universe.

"Can you tell me how you found me?" he asked.

"I got a visit from a couple of lieutenants who told me you were dead. Like a sentimental fool, I was gonna bury some of your favorite stuff with you, and when I opened the coffin, I saw a dummy, not you."

"Lucky for me that you were crazy enough to open the coffin. Then what?"

Grant dismissed the observation on his sanity and gave him a quick summary of what had happened since he'd started making calls, trying to find out what was really going on.

Mack swore again. "They really shot their own guy?"

"Yeah."

From the side of the room, Lily gasped.

Ignoring her reaction, he asked, "And how do you fit into that?"

"I was hired by the Phoenix Project to help run a program designed to give patients in comas a second chance. I was excited about our work."

"Looks like it got you into trouble," he said dismissively. "And you," he said to Grant with more feeling.

"The guys from the Roosevelt Memorial caught up with me at Hamilton Labs."

"It was Hamilton's idea to hide him in the VR," Lily said.

"And what happened after I left?" Grant asked.

"They held everybody at gunpoint while they looked for you, but they didn't figure it out."

Mack turned to Lily. "And what are *you* doing here?"

"I came back to help."

He might have said they didn't need her help, but it would have been a lie. Grant had sure as hell needed her to give him a stimulant to bring him around. On the face of it, that seemed weird. If this was a virtual reality, why would someone need a stimulant? But it was more proof that you could die in here under the wrong circumstances.

There were a lot of answers he could have given her. He chose to focus on the big picture.

"We've got to figure out what's going on with that hacker."

"Yes." She dragged in a breath and let it out. Landon is working on it from the other end."

"Who is he?" Mack asked.

"The programmer who designed this environment."

Mack gave a wry laugh. "Jesus, this is a hell of a place to wake up when you don't know what happened to you."

"He'd already gotten pretty far before I joined up. I take it he convinced Hamilton it was a good idea."

"He should have put us in a small American town. Something familiar."

"Wouldn't it have been just as weird in a small town with no people?"

"I suppose," Mack acknowledged, then gave her a direct look. "Maybe you should have come clean with everyone right away. That would have helped."

"Maybe. But the team agreed people needed an adjustment period."

"Or Hamilton wanted to see how they'd react," Mack shot back.

She shook her head. "I don't know. I signed on to the project to help people like my sister."

"Who somehow paid you a visit—only you were already back in the lab."

"Yes. And I called the facility where she's been for the past fifteen years. Her status hasn't changed. She's still in a coma there."

The conversation was interrupted by a knock on the door. "What the hell is going on in there?" a man's sharp voice called out.

It was Tom Wright who had gone in to try to get his e-mail earlier.

"We'll be out in a minute," Lily said.

Grant looked toward the door. "Who's that?"

"One of the patients you saw in those beds in the lab," Lily answered

"Yeah, and what are you planning to tell him and everybody else?" Mack asked.

"The truth."

"Even if some of them go crazy?" he asked.

"I think they've been here long enough that they'll accept the truth. But before we go out there, I need to tell you something." She looked from Mack to Grant and back again. "Dr. Hamilton, who runs the project, was in danger of running out of funding. Then someone named Avery Sterling came along and provided an infusion of cash. Hamilton claimed he investigated the guy before taking the money. I think he just wanted the cash and didn't look too closely."

"And what?" Grant asked.

"I think the goons who tried to kill you are working for Sterling, who wants to keep the project quiet."

"And he's willing to kill to keep it out of the news?" Grant asked.

Lily winced. "I wish it weren't true. But we've got another problem. Or maybe a clue to what's happening in here."

"Oh yeah?"

"I wasn't involved with the patients until the project was well under way. Maybe Hamilton initially thought he could handle the patients on his own. Then he decided he needed help. By the time I came on board, everyone was already here. Including someone Sterling asked Hamilton to include."

"Who?"

"I don't know. And I don't know why, either. Hamilton said it was a relative of Sterling's."

"It's a man or a woman?"

"He wouldn't tell me. He just said that it's a close relative of Sterling who was in an accident and needed to come in here to have a life, but I'm not sure that's true."

"Why not?"

"Because I think the hacker is after him—and why would he be?"

Mack shook his head. "Interesting question."

145

"I think we have to find out," Lily said.

Mack and Grant nodded.

Before they could continue the conversation, the pounding on the door resumed.

"This is ridiculous," the ski instructor called out. "If you don't open the door, I'm going to kick it in."

"Aggressive," Grant said.

She nodded. "He's been on edge since he got here." She looked back at the two brothers. "I'm going to open the door, and Mack's going to tell them about Hamilton Labs."

"Why not you?"

"Because you're the natural leader here."

He thought about that for a moment. "Okay. But I want backup from you if I need it."

"Of course," she said.

As soon as she turned the lock, the door burst inward and Wright charged in. Behind him, Mack could see the rest of the people he'd come to know here, all gathered for the big reveal. Some looked pissed that they had been excluded from whatever was going on in the business center. Others looked anxious. Paula was standing with her hands on her hips, glaring at him.

Wright's gaze zeroed in on Grant, then swung to Mack before settling on the newcomer. "Who the hell are you? I mean you look almost like him."

"I'm Mack's brother. His twin."

"And you just magically appeared here?" Wright demanded.

"It's complicated," Grant answered.

"You have to tell us what's going on," George Roper, the insurance agent, said.

"We will," Mack answered. "But why don't we all sit down," He gestured to the couches and chairs in the lobby.

"Let's go back to the bar," Jenny Seville, the teacher, said in a thin voice. "I mean, I feel better in a smaller space."

"Let's sit down *now,*" Roper demanded. "The sooner we get some information, the better."

There was a chorus of agreements, and Mack nodded. "Okay. But we can pull the sofas and chairs closer together."

Some of the men helped Mack and Grant move the furniture into a more compact grouping.

When Lily started to take a seat on one of the far sofas, he reached for her arm. "Sit next to me."

Her head whipped toward him, and he saw something in her eyes that made his stomach clench. It looked like she thought he was reaching out to her on a personal level when he actually wanted her as backup. She must have seen that on his face, because her own expression fell as she sat down next to him.

When the hotel guests were seated, Mack leaned forward. "I guess we should start with everyone introducing themselves to my brother."

"Why?" Wright asked.

"Like we did at the beginning," Mack answered. "He'd like to know who you are."

"I'm Paula Rendell," the travel agent started, and the others followed suit, some of them obviously not happy about the newcomer. Or maybe they thought Grant was a spy. For whom, exactly?

When they'd finished, Chris Morgan, the ski instructor, said to Grant, "Did you notice anything unusual about this place?"

"I couldn't afford to stay here," he quipped.

The line got a few laughs.

"So what do you do?"

Grant answered smoothly, "I'm a wilderness outfitter." That's what they'd helped their dad do in the summers, and Grant had gone back to it after leaving Decorah Security. He didn't mention that he'd also been with the CIA.

"You were going to give us some facts," Paula prompted, her gaze swinging back to Mack.

"Yeah, where are we, exactly?" Ben Todd, the lawyer, asked. He was one of the hostiles.

"Like Grant said, it's complicated," Mack responded.

"I'd appreciate a straight answer."

Mack had been thinking about what to say first. "This is going to sound weird, but everybody here is part of a medical experiment."

"How do you know?" George Roper demanded.

Mack glanced at Grant. "Because my brother found the lab that's conducting the experiment."

"This is a lab?" Roper shot back, looking around.

Mack shook his head. "Not exactly. The lab is in Maryland, and all of us are … sleeping there."

"Sleeping?" Chris Morgan, the ski instructor, bellowed. "Somebody put us to sleep. Like in that movie," he snapped his fingers. "What was it called?"

"Inception," Paula supplied.

"Yeah, like that."

Mack shook his head. "Similar, but not quite like that. Actually, everyone here was injured in some kind of accident. An accident that put each of us into a coma."

"Christ, you expect me to believe that," Roper growled, but Mack could see that wheels were turning in his head.

"It takes some getting used to. But when we said the last thing we remembered, it was usually just before an accident. Right?"

There were some reluctant nods around the room.

"The point is, back in the real world, we're severely injured."

"You're talking about yourself, too?" Paula asked.

"Yeah," he clipped out, wishing it weren't true. "In here, we can function normally."

Ben Todd slapped one hand against the sofa cushion where he was sitting. "There's nothing normal about this place. Like, for example, I can't taste anything."

"I think because of your particular brain injury," Mack answered.

"Brain injury," he said slowly, as though the reality were finally sinking in, at least for him. Others were looking like they hated the news.

"It's giving you a second chance," Grant said. "And you don't need to eat, anyway."

"Why not." several people asked.

"You have intravenous feed lines back in the lab," Grant said.

"Oh, goody," Roper muttered. "So you're saying we're not getting out of here?"

"You will, if you recover," Mack answered, knowing that at this stage, he had to give them some hope. "Meanwhile, you can do just about anything you want in here. And if stuff you want isn't currently available, it can be brought in," he added, hoping he wasn't lying.

The insurance salesman glared at Grant, "And what about your status?"

"I'm ... okay."

"Then what are you doing here?"

"I was looking for my brother."

Mack waited for another question about that and was relieved when nobody pressed him.

Instead, Roper demanded, "Back to the part you're skirting around. What are the chances of us getting out of here?"

CHAPTER TWENTY-ONE

Mack kept himself from glancing at Lily. He was sure she had a much more complete idea of the truth, but he'd already decided that the truth wasn't the best thing to throw at these people.

"We don't know," he said, then repeated what he'd explained before, hoping it would sink in. "But I was told this place is designed to provide us with as normal a life as possible."

"Who told you that?" Todd demanded. "What? You've had inside information from the first?"

"No."

"Then how do you know more than we do?"

"I talked to the doctor in charge."

"He was here?" Todd pressed, looking over his shoulder and glancing around, then shrugging.

"No." Mack gestured behind him. I was talking to Dr. Hamilton from the computer in the business center."

"And just how did you manage that?" Tom Wright chimed in. "I couldn't get the damn thing to work."

Grant spoke up. "It wasn't initiated from this end."

All eyes swung to him as he continued, "I was in the lab, looking for Mack. When I found out he was here, I asked to speak to him."

"And they just let you do it?" Roper shot back.

"I'm very persuasive."

Mack saw Lily roll her eyes.

Todd shifted in his seat. "So you expect us to believe all that crap?"

Lily spoke up for the first time. "You have a better explanation?"

He shrugged. "I'll let you know."

"God? The devil?" Paula said.

"Not unless he's wearing a white lab coat," Mack answered.

"Then what about the strange stuff that's happened? The weird sky. The guy you saw in the woods," Paula pressed. "Why would some doctor want any of that to happen—if this is supposed to be a normal environment?"

Mack sighed. "I was getting around to that." He looked at his brother. "You said that this place has been hacked."

"What do you mean, hacked?" Roper asked.

"Well, on a basic level, this is a computer simulation. Like a video game."

He could tell by the reactions that nobody liked the reminder.

"The guy who created the weird effects hacked in here."

"Who?"

"Apparently, someone named Preston. Anyone know him?" As he spoke the name, Mack watched for reactions around the room. He saw Grant and Lily doing the same thing.

"First name?" Todd asked.

Mack shrugged. "We don't know."

As far as he could tell, "Preston" didn't seem to register with any of them.

But maybe the guy was listening, because Mack's words were punctuated by a clap of thunder.

Some of the people in the group cringed or jumped. Most glanced up fearfully, although some of the guys looked back down almost at once. Mack saw Grant walk around in back

151

of the chairs and bend to put his arm around Jenny Seville. Apparently he'd been drawn to her as soon as he'd seen her.

"It's going to be okay," he murmured.

"How do you know?" she challenged.

"Because they're working on it back in the lab."

She nodded, looking grateful, and Mack hoped it was that simple.

He glanced toward Paula. "Is there an inside room where everybody could wait while I go outside and see what's happening?"

"The business center?" she asked.

"How about another office."

She pointed across the lobby toward an ornate desk. "There's an office behind it."

"Okay. Everybody can go in there," Mack said.

"Like a storm shelter?" Jenny asked.

"Yeah."

Todd snorted. "What good is that going to do?"

"So far Preston hasn't gotten in here. Let's assume that an interior room is safest."

As the others hurried toward the office, Grant hung back. "I want to see what's going on."

"It could be anything out there from a dragon to a squad of little blue men with ray guns."

"Let's go meet them."

Mack was torn as he considered his last encounter with Preston's effects. Grant was here as a volunteer. It wasn't fair to put him in danger.

"Okay," he finally agreed as he watched Lily usher people across the lobby. When everyone was inside, she turned to him, and he could tell from her face that she wanted to talk to him. Not about the situation here. About the two of them.

But there was no time for that now.

She must have been reading his face, too.

"Don't shut me out," she whispered.

He wasn't sure how to answer. That's exactly what he was doing on an emotional level because he didn't know if he could handle anymore disappointment.

"I'll be back as soon as I can," he said, avoiding the personal issue. When he started toward the exit they'd used to get to the bar, she turned and went into the office.

As Grant came up beside him. Mack couldn't stop himself from looking back at the closed door.

"You should give her a chance," he said.

"Why?"

"Because she cares about you," Grant answered.

"And you know that how?"

"By the way she looks at you. The way she talks to you."

"She made up a story to tell me and everyone else. She could have made an exception with me—after I fucked her," he spat out.

Grant winced. "That's how you think about it?"

"Okay. No. That's why I hate that she lied to me." There was a lot more he could have said, but he wasn't going to share his anguish with his brother.

Instead of pressing him, Grant said, "She was sent in here with a job to do. And did you ever consider that Hamilton may be using her right now?"

"What do you mean?"

"Maybe she's his control normal."

"Oh great."

He hadn't considered that perhaps her role in the research project might not be exactly what she'd assumed.

But that wasn't the most important thing he had to worry about. Keeping his voice low, he asked, "What's your opinion of the others?"

"With regard to what?"

"With regard to Lily's thinking that a ruthless killer named Avery Sterling might have special motives for putting one of them in here."

Grant winced. "If you put it that way, we should tie them up and start conducting our own interrogations."

"We don't have that option."

"Well, I haven't known them as long as you have. A lot of them are hostile. Like that Todd guy. And Roper and Wright."

"Yeah. But it would be nice to know if it's just because of the situation—or something unusual."

Another clap of thunder punctuated the conversation, and they picked up their pace.

"What if it's not what we think? What if one of the patients is working with the hacker?" Grant asked.

"I don't know," Mack said. "Why would they?"

Grant shrugged. "Hard to say without more information."

When they stepped into the courtyard, lightning flashed above them, followed by another thunderclap.

"The guy's in the woods," Mack said, pointing to the trees on the other side of the wall as he ducked into the covered walkway that skirted the lawn between the hotel and the wall. When they came to the end of the pavement, the door in the wall slowly opened. Mack braced for what might come out. This time it was a surge of red and gold flames that charred the wall as they curled around the edges.

"Jesus," Grant muttered as he tipped his head to the side, studying the effect. "Interesting. Can magic fire burn us?"

"Unfortunately, you have to assume it can. Like coming in here did a number on you until Lily gave you a stimulant."

As they watched warily, they saw vague figures moving in the flames, then something took more concrete form and rushed out, heading toward them, trailing fire. For the first time, Mack was seeing the hacker's effects break through into the hotel property.

In the woods he'd commanded a small army of hostile little men. Now his proxy had taken the form of a devil with horns on its head and a long, curved tail. It was bare-chested and wearing tight black pants. In its hand was a pitchfork, which it jabbed in their direction.

Mack and Grant both ducked back around the corner of the building, putting the wall between them and the ... *what?*

"Yeah, what?" Mack repeated.

Grant looked toward him. "You heard me say that—in my head?"

"I don't know. It was a natural question. Is it him taking that form, or is it a projection?"

"Maybe it doesn't make a difference."

Mack stopped talking and sent his brother a mental message. Grant looked toward him.

"Halloween costume devil," he said aloud.

"That's definitely what I was thinking," Mack answered. "Not very original. I guess I'm not worth the clever effects you told me about."

"Yeah. You're just a second-class resident," Mack agreed, trying to keep up the banter.

They both looked cautiously around the corner, and a wave of fire swept toward them, filling the air with acrid smoke and singeing their eyebrows.

"Cut it out," Mack shouted.

"Make me," a voice boomed.

"Why don't you just tell us what you want?" Mack suggested, trying to sound like you could have a reasonable conversation with this guy when every breath he took felt like it was burning his lungs.

"That's not the way the game works."

"It's not a game," Mack countered. "It's our lives."

"Such as they are." He paused. "Except for your brother and Dr. Wardman. They should get the hell out of here while they can."

"I like it here," Grant called back.

"Oh sure," the voice boomed, and for good measure, a large cloud of thick and nasty black smoke shot toward them. "Let's cut to the chase. I want the rest of the people out here so I can talk to them."

"Just talk?"

"Right."

"And then what?"

"Nothing bad."

"Oh sure," Mack answered. "Like nothing bad happened to me and Lily in the woods."

"That was just a taste of what I can do. If you don't cooperate, you're going to be sorry. As you can see, I'm getting more power over this place."

Mack winced, wishing it weren't true. But maybe he could give the guy a nasty jolt.

"Why don't you just tell us what you really want, Preston?" Mack called out.

The answer was a string of curses. "Where did you get that name?"

"Unfortunately for you, Shelly told me."

More curses.

"I guess it was a mistake sending her into Lily's room. But how did you manage it?"

"Like I'd tell you." Preston snorted. "She's just a stupid kid. I mean, she hasn't learned anything since she was five, has she?"

"Then what did you think you were going to get out of using her?"

There was no answer, but a shiver traveled over Mack's skin as a logical explanation for Shelly's visit grabbed him by the throat.

"What, Mr. Nice Guy? Did you think hurting her sister would persuade Lily to help you? But there was no way for it to work because Lily wasn't there when you sent the kid in."

"Fuck you."

Mack was pretty sure he'd figured out that nasty little part of the puzzle.

"Tell us what you want, and we might be able to help," he said.

"Like I believe that."

"Then stop messing with us," Mack growled.

"He's only got so much power," Grant whispered, "Or he'd be all over us." Mack was about to agree when the walkway under their feet started to crumble as though an earthquake had swept through the hotel grounds. Only the spot where they were standing was the only thing affected.

They leaped back, but Mack smashed into Grant who was too close behind him. He bounced forward off his brother's broad chest, lost his footing, and started falling into the gaping hole that had opened where the lawn and the sidewalk met. An involuntary scream welled in his throat when he saw the bubbling lava below him and felt the surge of heat licking at his legs.

CHAPTER TWENTY-TWO

Mack pictured himself plunging into the boiling lava and burning to a cinder.

Then he felt fingers tangle in the fabric of his tee shirt. It was Grant, stopping his downward plummet, then pulling him up.

Get back. You'll go in too, he shouted inside his head. But his brother's hands stayed in place.

He could feel the fabric starting to rip as he clawed at the sides of the pit. Dirt and rock broke loose and tumbled down, landing with sickening sucking sounds in the molten pool below. Mack knew he was going to follow them into the burning liquid.

No Grant silently shouted.

Mack looked around desperately and found a root sticking out from the side of the hole. As he grabbed for it, his fingers clawed at the wet surface, then gained some traction. He closed his fist and hung on to the projection, helping to stabilize himself. But not for long. He could feel the root slowly pulling out of the dirt as it sagged under his weight.

Before he went down, Grant gave a mighty heave, yanking him back to the surface. The two of them tumbled onto the paved walkway. Mack banged his elbow, but he and Grant both scooted back from the edge of the hole.

They were dragging in drafts of air as they watched the fault close up as though it had never been there.

Grant stared at the spot where the earth had opened up like a Florida sinkhole—with brimstone instead of water. "I guess you can get killed in here."

"I think so," Mack agreed as he stood up and brushed off his clothing. He'd thought his shirt was tearing, but it seemed to be okay now. Cole was also brushing himself off.

"I'm glad he didn't get you," a small voice said from the direction of the lobby.

They both turned to see Shelly standing on the walkway, dressed in the jeans and shirt she'd been wearing earlier.

Grant tipped his head to the side, studying her. "You're Lily's sister?" he asked. "The girl we were talking about?"

She nodded gravely. "I didn't know how nasty the Preston was. First I thought he was being nice bringing me here." Her face contorted. "Then I found out he didn't care about me."

"Unfortunately," Mack agreed. Instinctively he reached for her, and pulled her close.

She clung to him for long moments.

"I like you," she whispered.

"I like you too." He dragged in a breath and let it out. "I told Lily you were here, and she was sad that you left. She wants to see you."

"I want to see her. That's why I came back," she said, but she didn't sound entirely sure.

They all started for the main part of the hotel, with Shelly skipping ahead. When she reached the lobby, she stopped and looked around.

"Where is she?"

"I told her and the others to wait for us." He crossed to the office door and knocked. "It's Mack."

Lily opened the door. When she saw her sister, she rushed out, ran across the space that separated her from the little girl and caught her up in her arms, hugging her tightly as she swayed back and forth.

"Shelly! Oh Lord, Shelly, thank you for coming back. I'm so glad to see you."

Mack heard the tears in her voice, saw them in her eyes. Lily had said that this little girl was the reason she'd become a doctor, and he could understand that better now. She loved the sister who had been ripped away from her, and she'd grabbed at the chance to help other people who were in the same position.

"Me too," the child answered.

Lily set the little girl down, but kept hold of her hand, leading her to where the chairs had been pulled into a circle.

"I missed you," Shelly said.

"I've come to visit you a lot."

"Sometimes I could hear you."

"Good."

"I tried to see you, but I couldn't."

Mack and Grant had remained near the door of the office.

"I'll go in and tell them what happened," Grant said.

"Well, don't make it sound too scary," Mack advised.

"I think they have to be aware that the situation's changing. Especially those guys who are already on the edge of rebellion. Going outside could be fatal."

"Yeah, their best option is staying in the hotel."

"I'm not sure they believe it."

Mack nodded. "Right."

As Grant went into the office, Mack walked toward Lily and the girl. Remembering how his own encounter with Shelly had ended, he had a bad feeling about the meeting.

The little girl was talking. "When you visited me in the hospital, it wasn't the same as this. It always seemed like you were far away."

"Far away from what? I mean, where did it seem like you were?"

The little girl shivered. "In a dark place. It was boring. This place is much nicer."

"Yes."

"Can I stay here with you?" she asked in a plaintive voice.

Lily glanced toward Mack, a resigned expression on her face, and he knew she was thinking that was out of her control, at least until they got rid of the hacker.

He started toward them, just as the air around the girl rippled, and she vanished.

Lily leaped up, and reached for the spot where her sister had been. She gasped, then gave him a helpless look, tears in her eyes again.

"He gave both of us hope, then snatched it away. And now she's in a dark, awful place again," she whispered.

"Maybe not awful," he said.

"What else could it be?" she asked, sounding utterly defeated.

He didn't say what he'd figured out earlier—that it was lucky for Shelly and Lily that Preston still couldn't do much in the hotel proper.

Instead he said, "When this is over, you can bring her here and hook her into the system with the others."

"If it's ever over."

"It will be."

Mack had told himself he needed to distance himself from her emotionally. Now he knew that was impossible. Crossing the space between himself and Lily, he took her in his arms, feeling her shoulders start to shake. He could tell she was struggling not to break down, and he knew she was losing the battle.

Looking around, he saw other doors off the lobby. Because Lily needed to be alone, he picked her up and carried her to one of them. The first one he opened led to a supply closet. The second one opened into a small sitting room with a long couch and several overstuffed chairs.

He carried her inside, kicking the door closed behind him, then crossing to the couch where he sat down, cradling her in his lap.

She pressed her face to his chest and gave up the effort to keep from sobbing.

He caressed her back and ran his fingers into her hair, hoping he could make her feel better. As he stroked her, he kept speaking. "It's okay. We'll figure out how to get her over here on our terms—not his. She said she liked the hotel. She liked the ice cream. Even if she doesn't need to eat, she can enjoy the stuff any kid would want."

As he spoke, he felt Lily struggling for calm, and finally she wiped away the tears and raised her eyes to his with a look that made him flash back to when the earth had opened up under his feet.

"We don't know that. We don't even know how long this place is going to exist."

The words were like an icy knife plunging into his flesh. She was right. Hamilton could pull the plug any time he wanted. Or the other guy, the one who had provided the money. Or Preston could make it unlivable.

When Lily reached to clasp the back of Mack's head and pull his mouth down to hers, there was no thought of resistance. He had tried to tell himself that getting involved with her had been a mistake. Now he silently admitted that he'd felt like she was using him. And he'd been protecting himself by shutting her out.

It hadn't done him any good. He could feel an icy wind blowing at his back, reminding him that he might not have much time to enjoy what life he had left. But what time he did have he wanted to spend with Lily. The admission was like a giant weight being lifted off his shoulders.

He kissed her with a shocking desperation, as though she might be snatched away from him at any moment. Unfortunately it was true. If Hamilton wanted to bring her back to the lab, there was nothing stopping him from doing it.

And there was his own life to consider. It hung by a fragile cord that could be chopped in half at any time.

Not just by Hamilton. By the bastard named Preston who had hacked his way in here and was up to no good.

He pushed away those unwelcome thoughts as he turned his head one way and the other, feasting on the woman in his arms, feeling his desperation mirrored in her response to him. And when he wrapped her more tightly to himself and lay back on the couch, she came with him willingly, her body sprawling on top of his.

She raised her head, looking down at him.

"I was afraid I'd ruined everything."

"No."

"You were angry with me."

"I've got my head screwed on straight now."

"So do I," she breathed. "I want to be with you—so much."

He knew she was talking about now—and the future, which they might or might not have.

She brought her mouth back to his for more frantic kisses before lifting up and pulling off her sweat jacket and tee shirt. He reached around her, unhooking her bra and tossing it away, then made a low sound of pleasure as he took her breasts in his hands, loving the weight of them.

She arched into the caress, and when he stroked his thumbs across the hardened tips, she moved her sex against his erection, then cried out, her body going rigid.

When she flushed, he grinned up at her. "You came, just like that?"

"You don't mind?"

"Why should I?"

"I wanted you so much, I couldn't help it. But I didn't wait for you."

"But you have no idea how sexy it is to have a woman react to you that way."

Her flush deepened.

"Are you usually that quick on the trigger?" he asked, unable to keep from teasing a little.

"Never. It's you."

It was his turn to flush.

"You're a very potent guy."

163

"And you've reminded me to slow down and enjoy this. Not like last time when we were both too hot to wait."

He sat up and reached for his tee shirt, which he pulled off and tossed away. Then he turned back to her and tugged at her sweatpants and panties, dragging them down her legs.

She was naked now, and he stopped to admire her beautiful body as he began to stroke her, caressing her neck and collarbone, then sliding back to her breasts again before working his way down the front of her until he glided his hand into the swollen folds of her sex.

She kept her gaze on him, making a small sound of approval as he caressed her there, then dipped two fingers into her vagina, twisting them, watching the effect on her before he withdrew the fingers and stroked up to her clit, circling it gently.

"Oh Lord, Mack, you know how to do that."

"I want to make this good for you. As he caressed her so intimately, he watched the play of emotions on her face, awed by the way she had made herself vulnerable to him.

"I think I'm ready to try it the real way," she gasped out.

"That was real."

Neither of them said the obvious. That they were currently living in a fantasy environment. Yet what was happening between himself and this woman felt more vital than anything he could remember in his life.

She unzipped his jeans, reached inside and wrapped her hand around his penis, squeezing him in her fist, drawing a sound of pleasure from deep in his throat.

"You are so hard—and big."

"The better to nail you with, my dear."

She giggled, then pulled his pants down. When his cock sprang free, she leaned over to glide her tongue along his length, then took him into her mouth, the wet warmth pushing him toward the point of no return.

"I'm too hot for much of that," he managed to say, then forced himself to ease away. Lying back, he held out his arms.

"Let me see your gorgeous body above me when I'm inside you."

She accepted the invitation, straddling his hips and bringing his erection inside of her.

Their eyes locked as she began to move above him, slowly at first and then with more urgency, leaning forward to give herself maximum contact.

He had wanted the encounter to last, but once he was inside her, it was difficult to hold back.

He came in a blast of sensation, feeling her follow him before she collapsed on top of him.

He clasped her shoulders, stroking her, wanting to hold her in his arms forever.

"We'll make it work," she murmured, and he knew she was talking about the future they might have together.

"How?"

"I'll stay here with you."

"I think you'll have to go back to the lab and check up on Hamilton. At least sometimes. In here, you're as vulnerable as everyone else."

She sighed. "I know. But don't remind me of that yet. Let me be happy for a little while."

"Happy," he echoed. He'd given up on the idea of being happy long ago and settled for a job he loved. Now he felt a little spark of hope inside his heart, like the first flickers of flame when kindling catches. It could still go out, or it could spread and grow. He wanted that to happen so much, but he could hardly dare count on it.

Lily rolled to her side, then began searching around the floor and couch for her clothing. "In case someone comes in."

"Yeah, right."

He found his pants and pulled them on. When he reached to retrieve his shirt, she pressed her palm against his chest, and he looked up to see that she was half dressed. They both went still.

"I'm sorry," she whispered.

"For what?"

"For lying to you. For pretending to be one of the patients—when you kept giving me opportunities to come clean with you."

"I understand," he said quickly, perhaps too quickly.

"Do you?"

"You were committed to the project. Hamilton convinced you that you had to play the role he assigned to you in here."

"I should have done more thinking for myself, but I was excited that Hamilton had chosen me for the team. There were a lot of candidates, but he picked me."

"Because you're good."

"And maybe because he knew he could keep me focused on his plans."

She turned away and found the rest of her clothing.

"What would you have done differently?"

"Told them the truth about this place," she said with jerky movements as she dressed.

"You don't think they would have freaked out?"

"Well, I wouldn't have blurted it out. I would have eased into it. Preston kind of made that impossible for me—or anyone else. On the other hand, he made it easy to believe that the Hotel Mirador is some kind of super video game."

"Yeah." He swallowed hard. "Are you sorry about this?"

He heard her voice go soft, like an old fashioned lacy valentine. "Making love just now? Absolutely not. You don't know how relieved I was that you still wanted me."

"I never stopped."

"But you were angry."

"Yeah."

She reached for him, clasping him in her arms, and he did the same. They held each other for a few moments before he asked the question that had been churning inside him.

"Do you think I can get out of here?'

He heard her swallow hard. "From the first, I thought you had a good chance of recovery. You had a good Glasgow Coma Scale."

"What's that?"

"A test we administer to patients in a coma. You get a numerical score for things you can do, like open your eyes, make sounds, respond to painful stimuli. The scale goes from three to fifteen. You were up to twelve. I told Hamilton you shouldn't be here, but I think he'd already gone to a lot of trouble to get you."

"Right. He stole me."

She made an angry sound. "I believe he thinks this project is going to make him a superstar in the field of coma treatment. Too bad he has no scruples about how he accomplishes his goals."

He nodded, then said, "You were handicapping my chances."

"You were always different from the other patients. You were always responsive to me. I knew I was getting ... attached to you. Then when we all woke up here—there you were, the man I'd been longing to meet. And there's another good sign. After I came back to the lab and Grant was there, you responded to both of us. You opened your eyes, looked at us, and said something."

He thought about that. "Maybe I remember. I mean I remember something strange happening before I talked to Grant on the monitor. It was like this world faded around me."

"Yes."

He hung on to her, longing to reassure her that they'd figure a way out of this situation for the two of them, but he couldn't get the words past the lump in his throat. And he couldn't say something that might turn out to be a lie.

CHAPTER TWENTY-THREE

Mack forced himself to focus on solving the current problem. "We have to go back and join the group."

"And what?"

"You said someone in here isn't who we think they are. We have to figure out who it is—and why."

She spread her hands helplessly. "But how?"

"Too bad there's not some kind of test we can administer. Did any of them strike you as 'off'?"

She laughed. "To use a technical term, most of them are kind of weird."

"Right. I keep wondering if Tom Wright is lying about his background. And it's pretty clear that Jenny Seville is hiding something." As he spoke, another thought struck him. "Didn't Hamilton have patient records that gave their background?"

She dragged in a breath and let it out. "Yes. I asked for that, and he gave me detailed records, but now I don't know if they were real. I mean he could easily have changed their names and how they'd gotten injured. He could have changed anything in their backgrounds."

"Great."

She went on. "There was a lot of information on you. I copied your file and brought it home."

"Oh yeah?"

She flushed. "I was praying you'd get better."

He wanted to proclaim that he would. He didn't bother with the affirmation. Either it would be true or not.

"Now I'm thinking others could have been stolen for the project. Only their relatives didn't open a closed casket like your brother did."

"I hope Grant doesn't regret it."

"Why would he?"

"He's gotten himself into trouble. Here and in the real world." He glanced toward the door, then back at Lily. "When we were out there, we saw a devil."

"What do you mean a devil?"

"A creature that looked like a devil, with a tail and horns. Wearing black tights and hurling fire. It was either a projection like the things in the woods, or it was Preston himself in that persona. This time he had a lot to say."

"What?"

"He demanded that everyone come out on the lawn. When we said it wasn't gonna happen, he made the earth open up onto a pit of boiling lava. I almost went in, but Grant grabbed me."

She gasped, reaching for him and holding tight again. "Oh my God."

"Unfortunately, this time Preston came through the gate and onto the lawn. And the pit was at the edge of the hotel."

She made a low sound of distress. "That's bad."

"Yeah. I'm surer than ever that we can really get hurt—or killed—in here."

"I didn't think so when Hamilton described the protocol. I've changed my mind," Lily said.

"Just because of Preston?"

"I don't know. I thought the designer, Sidney Landon, knew what he was doing. At least he sounded pretty awesome when he described the environment to me. Now I know there are too many unknowns to be sure of anything, at least with Preston assaulting the program."

"Then we have to be careful."

"Unfortunately, we don't even know what the dangers are until they happen."

He nodded, then glanced toward the door. "I'm thinking we might want to go upstairs and look out my bedroom window. It's got a view of the grounds and the woods beyond. Maybe we can see what Preston's up to now."

"Good idea," she agreed.

"But I want to let Grant know."

They both walked into the lobby and crossed to the room where they'd left the others. When Mack knocked on the door, Grant called out, "Who is it?"

"Santa Claus," Mack answered.

His brother opened the door and gave them a long look. "Everything okay?"

"Yes."

Mack studied the faces turned toward him. Most looked worried, but Grant had apparently done a good job of keeping the panic down to a manageable level.

"We thought we might ...," he stopped talking aloud and finished the rest of the sentence in his mind, sending it to Grant.

His brother's eyes widened. Then he looked up.

Mack felt a spurt of elation. Once again, his brother had heard him. At least something good had come out of getting stuck in a computer game. He and Grant were reestablishing the silent communication that they'd shared when they were kids. Or was it only because his body was asleep in a lab, and his mind had an unaccustomed freedom? He hoped that wasn't the reason.

"Do what?" Tom Wright, the car salesman, asked from where he stood with his shoulder propped against the wall. When Mack had first seen him, he'd seemed pretty laid back. Now he seemed to be struggling to maintain that posture, under the pressure of the attacks from Preston.

"I'd rather not say," Mack answered. "In case Preston's listening."

"Then how does your brother know?"

"Sometimes we read each other's minds."

"Yeah, right."

Mack shrugged. "We'll be back in a little while."

"I'm tired of being cooped up in here," the car salesman, if that's what he really was, said.

There were murmurs of agreement.

Wright started for the door and pushed past Mack into the lobby where he looked around like he expected to find that Mack and Lily were hiding a nasty surprise from the rest of them.

Roper and Todd marched out after him like little boys who were determined to get their share of whatever privileges were being handed out. The women were not as quick as the men to leave the sheltered area. But Paula Rendell stepped through the doorway and looked around. Mack glanced at Lily, and she gave him a look that said, "We can't force them to play it safe."

The rest of the group had trailed out, although Jenny Seville stayed near the door. Grant moved to her side and put his arm around her.

She gave him a grateful look.

"Stay in the hotel," Mack warned.

"Maybe," Roper answered.

Persistence had paid off. That last blast of energy with the devil fire had burned a hole in the barrier between Danny Preston and the hotel grounds. Now he stood with his eyes closed, a look of deep concentration on his face as he aimed a life energy field meter at the hotel wall. He figured it was as good a device as any for pulling thoughts from the hotel guests whose privacy he hadn't already invaded.

When he clicked off the meter, a broad grin spread across his face. He would have whooped in triumph, except that he still wanted to conceal his presence for a little while longer.

He wasn't going to go sneaking in there. He was going to make sure he entered as Caesar returning to Rome after conquering Egypt.

He'd scanned the minds of everyone inside the hotel, excluding Bradley and Wardman because he'd already done them. He hadn't been able to probe the others as deeply as those first two, because he wasn't doing it face to face, so to speak. But he'd gotten enough to know which guest was the one he'd been sent here to interrogate.

He turned and headed back to his base of operation, planning the details of his grand entrance.

"Back soon," Mack said. Before Wright or anyone else could ask more questions, he turned toward the steps.

He and Lily climbed the broad stairs to the second-floor hallway. As he reached the landing, he looked around at the patterned wallpaper, the thick carpet, the marble balustrade. This place was as elegant as a palace—and could be his home for the rest of his life. If you were objective, it wasn't such a bad living environment. And think of the advantages. You could have anything you wanted to eat—assuming the kitchen was open, and you would never get fat. On the other hand, he didn't like looking over his shoulder all the time waiting for Preston to pull a new trick,

He glanced at Lily and caught her watching him.

"Maybe I can read your mind—like your brother."

"Yeah. If I have to stay here, we're going to have to talk to Landon about what food to stock," he quipped. "Even if we don't really need it."

"For the record, I'm an excellent cook. I love coming home and fixing something good."

He would have liked to stand there talking about making the environment more livable, but he had come upstairs for a reason. Turning, he started rapidly down the hall to his room, knowing Lily was having trouble keeping up.

His key was in his pocket. He might have thought he'd lost it, but maybe it always came back to the pocket like a homing pigeon when you were out and about.

When he'd opened the door, they stepped into the sitting room. Lily reached for his hand, and he knitted his fingers with hers.

"Too bad we don't have time for anything besides business," she whispered.

"Maybe a little bit of time," he answered, swinging her around and wrapping her in his arms as he lowered his mouth to hers. He'd thought it would be a quick kiss. It lasted longer than he intended, and when they finally broke apart, they were both breathing hard, and his erection was straining against her middle.

He held her for a moment longer, wanting more but knowing that was impossible now.

Finally, he eased away. "Sorry."

"For what?" she asked.

"That I can't take you in the bedroom right now and fuck your brains out."

She laughed. "That's how you think about it?"

"At the moment—yes."

A flash of movement outside the window caught his attention, and he tried to snap his mind back to business as he looked out. He'd thought he'd seen a bird. Instead it was a blue- and silver-winged creature with a long snout that looked like a trumpet. In fact, the instrument was blasting away triumphantly, playing Beethoven's Ode to Joy slightly faster than the usual tempo.

Mack crossed to the window as he took in the view below. "What the hell?"

Lily followed.

There were several of the creatures flying in a circle above the open area of the lawn, blasting their loud music, and the door in the wall was wide open.

173

As Mack and Lily watched, the man they'd seen in the tree came through. He was dressed like a biker again. In fact, he was riding a honking big red and chrome bike that gouged a muddy tire track as it crossed the lawn. Behind him marched a contingent of the little men Mack had seen earlier, ammunition belts slung across their chests like old-time Mexican soldiers. They all held automatic weapons in firing position, as though they were ready to fight off a screaming mob—not a group of unfortunate patients trapped in the hotel lobby.

Mack struggled to draw in a full breath as he tried to comprehend what was happening. "Jesus, he's figured out how to get all the way in here."

The biker stopped on the lawn, cocking his head to the side as though listening to something only he could hear. After a few moments, he pulled out his cell phone and made a call. It was very brief, but he looked like he'd won a victory as he put the phone away.

"What was that all about?" Lily asked.

"I don't know. I'm guessing he was making a report to someone."

"Sterling?"

"That's my best guess. We have to go down and warn the others that he's gotten onto the grounds."

He charged back to the door, and turned the handle, but it seemed to be locked from the outside.

"Jesus," he said again. "He must have seen us up here. He wants to keep us from going down and telling anyone what's happening."

Mack looked toward the phone on the desk.

"Too bad it doesn't work," Lily said, answering his unspoken question.

They both turned back to the window and stared down again. The honor guard of little warriors was marching after Preston as he headed for the entrance by the bar.

174

Mack tried the door again. When it wouldn't open, he cursed and looked around for a battering ram. He picked up the heavy, carved desk chair, lifted it over his head and smashed it at the door. The first time it bounced off, but he kept lifting and smashing, and finally he'd made a hole large enough to reach through. Fumbling for the keycard again, he managed to angle his hand around and swipe the plastic through the slot.

The door whizzed open, almost hitting him in the face as he worked the mechanism.

"Come on," he shouted to Lily.

They both raced down the carpeted hall and pounded down the marble steps, but before they reached the main floor, Mack could already see it was too late. He stopped short, taking in the scene in the lobby.

Preston had driven right inside, the bike leaving a nasty brown streak across the beautiful Oriental carpet.

People tried to scatter as the hacker drove toward the center of the group. But the fully-armed men lowered their automatic weapons, training them on the group.

Grant was still trying to herd people back into the smaller room, but a couple of warriors blocked the way.

Preston sprang off his motorcycle, propped it against one of the marble columns in the lobby, and reached for Paula Rendell who had apparently lost the ability to move.

That changed as he grabbed her. She started flailing, and he shook her hard.

"Cut it out."

"Let go of me."

Ignoring the plea, he turned her back to his front. When she was secure in his clutches, he pulled out a curved knife with a jeweled handle and flourished it in the air before pressing the edge of the blade against her throat.

She screamed.

"Shut up," he ordered.

She quieted, her eyes wide with terror as she looked around at the crowd. They stared back in horror.

"I'm going to cut to the chase. Bring me George Roper," Preston ordered, "or I kill her."

"George Roper?" Mack asked. He could see Preston's look of triumph that he'd finally gotten some control of the situation in the VR. But Mack could also see his desperation. He hadn't been mounting these attacks on a whim. He was on an important mission.

Was he going to get into bad trouble if he didn't accomplish his goal, whatever it was? It would have been easy to say he was just crazy. He was exhibiting behavior you could call insane. Specifically megalomaniac. But there had to be method behind his madness. He'd gone to a lot of trouble to get into this place. All to grab George Roper?

"How do you know you want Roper?" Mack called down.

"I've eliminated everyone else."

"What do you want with him?" Mack pressed.

"You don't need to know." Preston turned his attention to the crowd in the lobby, his expression hopeful as he scanned the faces.

Everybody else was doing the same thing.

"Roper's not here," Todd finally said.

"What do you mean—not here?" Preston said. "There's nowhere he can go."

Grant moved back toward the room where he'd kept the patients quiet. His brother came out moments later and shook his head.

"He's not in there."

Preston made a sound of frustration. "When was the last time you saw him?"

"I think he came in here with everybody else," Grant said. "But then he and some of the others walked out."

"Find him."

"Why is he important?" Mack tried again.

"You think I'm going to tell you?"

"But you're sending us around the hotel to search?" Mack asked.

"Like you said, there's nowhere to go but in here."

Roper could go into the woods, but he'd be a fool to do it after what he'd heard from Mack.

He nodded. "We should keep to the buddy system."

"Why?" Preston snapped.

"Safer."

The hacker laughed. "There's nothing gonna hurt you in here, except me."

"Or Roper. He could assault anyone who catches up with him."

"Fair point," Preston conceded.

Assuming that sticking with Lily was going to be okay, Mack clasped her hand, leading her back the way they'd come. At the same time, he was frantically sending a message to his brother.

Meet me in room 250. Meet me in room 250.

He couldn't be sure the message was getting through, but he kept a tight hold on Lily as they climbed the stairs.

Neither one of them spoke while they were within sight of the man who held Paula. When they turned the corner in the hall, Lily finally spoke.

"Where are we going? I mean, he's right; we can't get out of here."

"Um—that's not exactly true. You left, using that thing in your closet."

She gave him a wide-eyed look. "How do you know?"

"That was the only logical explanation for your disappearing. And I'm hoping Grant will come up here."

They reached her door, and she fumbled in her pocket for her key.

When they'd stepped inside, he left the door ajar.

"Okay, what are we doing?" she asked.

"You're going back to the lab. Then you're bringing me back there and waking me up."

She caught her breath. "I can't let you do that. You ... might not be able to function without life support outside the VR."

"You said I already woke up."

"Very briefly. There are layers of consciousness."

"You said there was a good chance I could recover."

"Yes, but we can't just jump in with both feet."

"I think we have to."

When the door opened, they both tensed, but it was Grant, who had gotten the mental communication.

"What?" he asked.

"We're all going back to Hamilton Labs."

"What do you mean—we?"

"Just what it sounds like."

His brother's reaction was the same as Lily's. "Not you!"

"Something's going on there that we have to figure out," Mack said.

Grant looked at Lily, "Even if he can wake up, what kind of physical shape will he be in?"

"Under ordinary circumstances, a patient who's been in bed for weeks can't just get up and walk around without help. But that special bed will have kept him flexible and kept him from getting bedsores. Plus he's been getting regular physical therapy for his muscles," she answered, then added, "But I wouldn't recommend just trying to bring him back to full consciousness. His neck—"

"Was twisted," Mack finished. "And I've had time to heal. You said I was responding to you."

She gave him a helpless look. "You could die."

"I'm betting I won't."

"It's a bet I don't want to make."

"I'm the one making it, and it's got to be done," he said. "Open the closet, and show him."

She sighed and went to the touchpad.

"It's my birthday, she said. 4, 30."

"Okay."

After she'd pressed the right code, she opened the door, revealing the hidden equipment.

Grant looked torn, then said, "I'm going to stay here. If we both leave, the others will be unprotected."

"You mean Jenny will be unprotected," Mack said.

Grant gave him a startled look. "You noticed."

"Yeah."

Lily crossed to the machinery and activated a control. A screen appeared with a picture of the lab. They could see Hamilton and another man Mack hadn't seen before. The visitor to the lab was taller than average with a trim build, dressed in dark slacks, a white shirt and a conservatively cut dark leather jacket in a conservative cut. He moved like a man in his forties, but he had white hair and lined features that made him look like he could be older.

Two other hard-faced men stood by the door but didn't join in the conversation.

"Can they see and hear us?" Mack asked as he watched Hamilton and the other guy. Even without the sound turned on, Mack could tell that Hamilton was on the defensive with the visitor.

"No," Lily answered.

"Who's he talking to?"

"Sterling," Lily said. "The big shot who came in with the funding. He had several meetings here." As they watched, he walked over to one of the beds and looked down at the patient.

"Who's that?" Mack asked.

"Roper," Lily answered.

179

CHAPTER TWENTY-FOUR

"Mack nodded. "Figures. It's not just Preston who is interested in Roper. He must be the guy Sterling paid Hamilton to put in there."

Lily had turned on the sound from the lab, and they heard the men talking.

"I paid you to keep him alive in there," Sterling said, his voice hard as glass.

"And I've held up my part of the bargain," Hamilton answered.

"Have you? I think you're hiding something."

"Of course not."

"I want to talk to that hotshot programmer of yours. What's his name?"

"Landon, and he's busy."

"Doing what?"

"Keeping the place running."

"Doesn't it run by itself?"

"There are always little adjustments."

"Let's go talk to him."

Panic flashed on the doctor's face, but apparently he didn't feel he was in a position to refuse.

"I'll tell him we're coming."

"No. Well just walk in and see what's going on up there."

Hamilton looked like he wanted to argue—or throw up. Instead he headed for the door.

Mack's breath was shallow until Hamilton and the two thugs had left with Sterling.

"I'm not sure how much time we have," he said to Lily. "You'd better go in there while you have the chance."

She gave him a tight nod.

"How long does it take?"

"It happens right away," she answered, looking like she was on the edge of panic, then made an effort to get control of herself as she glanced at Grant. "Except that I had Landon wait to send you in so I could be here when you arrived. But going back, it's immediate."

"Okay."

She gave him a direct look. "You're sure you want to follow me?"

"Yes. But ... "

"But what?"

He didn't want to entertain the possibility that he was living the last few minutes of his life, but he had to be realistic. He was in this VR environment because his bailout had put him in a coma.

"If I don't make it, you have to get out of the lab."

"And what?"

Grant spoke. "And contact the organization I used to work for. Decorah Security. They're in Beltsville. Tell Frank Decorah everything. He'll help you."

"Frank Decorah," she repeated the name and the phone number he gave her, then glanced at Mack.

"Yeah, that's an excellent idea. Everything I've heard about Decorah Security is good."

"Okay."

"Let's get this show on the road, before the thug and your boss come back. Or maybe they're all thugs."

Lily nodded. "Landon made it pretty simple for me to get back." She swept her hand toward the interior of the portal, which was about the size of an old-fashioned telephone booth. "You stand against the back wall, then press this button."

He watched where she pointed.

She was about to step inside the device. Instead she turned and reached for Mack, pulling him into her arms and holding tight.

He made a strangled sound, clinging to her for heartbeats. They could be saying good-bye, he thought, with a sudden tightening of his chest. He prayed not, because that would mean one of them was dead—probably him.

Another thought struck him. Hamilton and Sterling could come back and catch her in the midst of acclimating herself to the real world.

"You'd better go," he whispered.

"I know."

"How long before I can follow you?" he asked.

"You can see me on the screen. I'll get out of bed, then tell you to come on." Her voice rose as she said the last part, and he knew she was worrying about his making it back.

"Okay. Better do it while we've got the chance."

She was about to step to the machine, when he said, "Wait."

"What?"

"Is there a weapon in the lab, in case I need it?"

"Mine," Grant said.

"I put it in the desk drawer," Lily answered.

"Okay."

Stiffly she stepped into the machine, closing the door behind her.

Mack's heart started to pound as he imagined her winking out of existence like in the Star Trek transporter room. Maybe it was something like that, because in the VR, her body was only an electronic representation of her real self. Like his own current body.

As he heard equipment whirring, he kept his gaze fixed on the computer screen. Lily had been here moments earlier. Now she might as well be on another planet. Again he thought of the Star Trek transporter.

The sides of the beds blocked his view of the patients. Then one of the sleepers reached a hand over the rail, a small feminine hand.

"Lily?" he whispered. "Let me know you're okay, sweetheart."

As though she heard him, she sat up and looked toward the monitor, then shot her gaze toward the door before she took off the cap she was wearing and started pulling leads and wires from her body.

She grasped the side of the bed, glancing around like she was having the same science-fiction reaction as Mack. She'd gone from here to there in the blink of an eye. He knew she'd done it before. Was it different for her now because of their relationship? He struggled to put the relationship idea out of his mind. She couldn't have a real *anything* with a guy in a coma

She stayed where she was for a few moments, then looked toward the door to the lab again before standing up. As she did, he saw relief flood her face.

Turning toward the computer screen, she said, "They're gone. Give me a minute to get dressed."

He watched while she crossed the room to a cabinet, where she pulled out a scrub suit, then took off her hospital gown and shoved it onto the bottom shelf before dressing.

He saw her take a deep breath before looking toward him. "Come on."

"Here goes nothing," he answered.

After embracing Grant, he broke away. He didn't have to read Grant's mind to know his thoughts.

"I'm gonna be okay," he said, hearing the thickness in his own voice.

"I almost didn't make it here," his brother answered. "I needed Lily to help me."

"She's already waiting for me. You go down and make sure Preston doesn't do too much damage."

"When I know you're safe."

He wanted to tell Grant the people in the lobby needed him, but he only turned and stepped into what he had come to think of as the transporter.

He had assumed he would be in the dark once he closed the door, but there was a warm glow emanating from hidden lights along the ceiling. He could see the button Lily had showed him. It was also faintly glowing. As soon as he looked at it, he realized they wouldn't want you fumbling around in here when the door was closed.

Before he could change his mind he reached out and stabbed it with his finger.

He felt a sensation like a mild electric current coursing through his body, and then he was nowhere.

From the screen in the VR, Grant watched what was happening in the lab. Lily was anxiously hovering over one of the beds. Mack's bed, he presumed.

She was looking down at the patient, speaking in a low voice. Then she looked at the screen.

"Is he all right?" Grant shouted.

"I don't know," she answered. "This may have been a very bad idea."

"Christ, no," he whispered under his breath, wanting to shout the words but knowing that might call Preston's attention to his location.

"Save him," he said.

"You stayed to help the people in there. Go do it," Lily said.

"No."

"You can't do anything here. And you're just distracting me." She sounded angry, probably because Mack had put himself in danger, yet she couldn't direct her *anger toward him.*

As she spoke she turned back to Mack, her whole focus on him.

She'd told Grant there was nothing he could do. But maybe he could help get through to his brother.

Mack he shouted inside his mind. *Mack wake up.*

CHAPTER TWENTY-FIVE

Mack sensed that someone was calling his name, urgently, insistently—but from far away so that he could barely hear. Was it his brother? Or was it Lily? Or both of them? And what was he going to do about that?

"Mack, can you hear me, Mack? Oh Lord, Mack, answer me. Please answer me."

He could tell that voice was Lily's. He heard his brother, too. Silently calling him. But she was closer now, and he knew she was worried about him.

Still, he was confused. Hadn't he been flying an F18 fighter jet that was hit? And he'd had to eject.

No, that was years ago.

No, it couldn't be years. That was impossible. He remembered it like it was yesterday.

And then ...

He struggled to make sense of the next part.

He'd ended up in the VR. That's where he'd met Lily and made love with her.

That last piece of information jolted him.

Or was someone shaking his shoulder? His head swam in confusion. It felt like his body and his mind were detached, and he couldn't bring the two of them together no matter how hard he struggled.

"Mack. For God's sake, Mack. Wake up. You have to wake up. Hamilton and that other guy could come back any minute."

Another piece of information that slithered through his mind—in one side and out the other. He grabbed at the snake's tail before it was completely gone.

Did he know someone named Hamilton? What was she talking about?

"Open your eyes and look at me!"

Her voice had been soft and gentle. Suddenly it was sharp and commanding.

He tried to tell her he only wanted to go back to sleep. Then he felt a needle stabbing into his arm.

Seconds later, a bolt of sensation surged through him, and he gasped. His body was on fire, every nerve screaming, and all he knew was that he had to get away.

His eyes blinked open, and his hands clawed at the rails that confined him as his panic threatened to wipe out all reason.

"Mack! Please, Mack."

He tried to zero in on the voice and the face hovering above him, but it was just too hard to concentrate. He wanted to go back to sleep.

"Mack, it's Lily. Please, Mack."

Then he heard her gasp.

He was aware of movement as she sprang away from him.

Moments later, another voice said, "What's going on here?" It was a man who sounded like he'd been taken by surprise, and now he expected the right answers.

Another man cleared his throat and said, "This is my associate, Dr. Lily Wardman."

"Where were you earlier?" the first man said.

There was a long pause. Finally Lily said, "I was in the VR."

"What?" the first man asked as though he was in total shock. "How is that possible?"

"I've been going in periodically to make sure the program is running smoothly," Lily answered.

"Oh, have you?" the questioner asked. "Does that mean you've talked to them?"

"Some of them," she admitted.

Grant had stayed in the VR to help the patients. Lily had told him to go do his job. Knowing there was nothing he could do for Mack, he'd left her room and headed back toward the common area. Now he stood at the corner of the hallway where he could look down on the lobby with minimal risk of being seen.

It looked like nothing much had changed. Well, Preston had apparently gotten tired of holding on to Paula. She was sitting on the floor, hugging her knees and gasping. But he saw no blood, thank God.

The little warriors were aiming automatic weapons at the people who had returned to the lobby—apparently without finding Roper. Grant thought about fading back around the corner and heading down the hallway. But Preston was right about his options. There was nowhere to go beyond the hotel. And he'd stayed here to watch out for Jenny.

He located her in the crowd. She was sitting hunched on one of the side chairs, her hands gripping her shoulders and her head bowed.

She looked like she wished she could turn herself inside out and disappear.

His chest tightened as he watched her. They'd talked a little bit in the office when they'd been hiding out. He knew she was in some kind of serious trouble, but she didn't trust him enough to tell him what it was.

He was going to get her to level with him, but he didn't have the luxury of a long conversation with her now. Or any conversation, until they took care of the Preston problem.

Grant dragged in a breath and let it out. As soon as he stepped around the corner, the biker spotted him.

"Ah, one of the Bradley twins. Come on down," he called, sounding like the guy who used to run that TV program, The Price is Right.

Grant started down the stairs.

"Nice of you to join us again," Preston said, his voice dripping with sarcasm. "Did you find Roper?"

"No."

"Then what were you doing up there?"

"Looking for him," he answered as he reached the ground floor.

"I don't think so. You left with your brother and Lily. Where are they?"

"We split up," Grant said.

"Yeah, I see that. Let's find out if I can get some straight answers out of you."

Suddenly ropes materialized in the air. They flew toward Grant, circling his body, dragging him against one of the pillars and binding him to the column.

Preston walked over, studying him.

"I'm thinking I can persuade you to talk," he said in a voice that made Grant's flesh crawl.

The hacker reached out a hand that had turned into a claw and ripped open the front of Grant's tee shirt. The action drew gasps from the other people in the lobby.

Then Preston spread the torn sides apart, exposing Grant's chest. The man's hand had become normal again. And now he was holding some kind of plastic box. It had wires attached, with metal clips.

Preston attached a clip to each of Grant's nipples. Then he stepped back and inspected his handiwork before turning a dial on the box he held. Electric current zinged down the wires, delivering a jolt that made Grant struggle not to scream. Preston turned up the current, and Grant couldn't hold back a gasp.

But his gaze was defiant as he met Preston's inquiring gaze.

"That's not going to make you talk?" he asked.

"Hell no."

"Hum, then what about this?"

There was a whir of motion several feet away. Jenny screamed as the same kind of ropes materialized out of the air, wrapped around her and bound her to another pillar.

"Leave her alone," Grant shouted.

"Yeah, like I figured, you care what happens to her."

"You bastard."

As Preston had done before, he reached out a claw and ripped Jenny's shirt open, then her bra. The hand turned back into its normal form as he pushed the remains of Jenny's tee shirt and bra to the side and fondled her breasts.

People in the room gasped.

"Leave her alone," Grant shouted again, desperately struggling to free himself. But the ropes held him in place against the pillar. Grant hadn't known Jenny long, but something in her had called to him. She was so sweet and vulnerable. And he could see she didn't give her trust easily. Now he could see he'd gotten her into this terrible position.

Preston turned back to him with a smile on his face. "I gave you a taste of what that electric current felt like. How do you think it's gonna feel on her?"

Mack lay in his bed struggling to stay away and also struggling to understand what was going on around him.

A man was talking to Lily, his voice low and nasty.

"Perhaps we should have a discussion about your contact with the patients," he said.

"I really have work to do," Lily responded, obviously struggling to keep her own voice even.

"Well, technically, you're working for me, since I'm funding the project," the man said, his tone sending a chill over Mack's skin.

"Yes, I know."

Mack struggled to make sense of the conversation. The man who had funded the project was ... Sterling. This must be him. But what was he doing here?

"Do you know why I stepped in?" he asked.

"No," she answered, but Mack could hear the hesitation in her voice.

"I think it would be a good idea for us to have a chat," Sterling said.

"I should check the patients."

"Later," the man snapped. "We're going to talk. You, me, Hamilton and the designer of the program."

"But ...

"You're lying about something, and we're going to find out what's going on."

"No."

He heard the sound of a hand slapping flesh, and she cried out in pain and surprise.

"Now," the man shouted.

"Leave her alone," Hamilton said, but his voice was thin and watery.

"Shut up and get going."

Mack heard the sound of people moving off. Then a door shut.

Jesus! The man had hit Lily—right in front of Dr. Hamilton. Which meant there was no telling what else the guy was going to do. And there was no one to help her but Mack.

That terrible knowledge started his heart hammering. It also helped clear his brain. He'd felt foggy. Now the fog was lifting. He wanted to leap out of the bed, but he knew that leaping was way beyond his present condition. Maybe getting up at all.

No. He had to get up—and save Lily from the bastard who had hit her.

His eyes opened, and he blinked in the sudden brightness. He was staring up at one of those tile ceilings where a metal grid holds the panels in place and some of the tiles are replaced by light panels.

He'd wanted to be left alone so he could sleep off what felt like a two-day drunk. Now he knew he had to get himself up and find Lily before Sterling did something worse to her.

He dragged in a breath and let it out before reaching for the rails at the side of the bed. Cautiously he pushed himself up, feeling a wave of dizziness sweep over him. He fought the urge to lie back down and rest—just for a little while. Instead, he waited for the sensation to pass. He knew that if he moved, he was going to throw up. But he had to push past that. For Lily.

Gritting his teeth, he willed his stubborn body to accept that he was awake and intended to function in the real world.

The rails on the sides of the bed were in his way, and he didn't know how to lower them. Instead he scooted toward the end of the bed, until some kind of line attached to his arm stopped him. He looked up, seeing a drip bottle that led to the tube inserted in his arm. Not knowing what else to do, he pulled it out, seeing fluid spill out onto the floor.

Every motion seemed to take forever to complete, but finally he was standing on unsteady feet.

He had to grip the end of the bed to stay upright. How long had he been lying there? He didn't really know. He'd thought it might be years, but it couldn't be that long. Weeks or months, more likely.

Lily had said the bed and physical therapy had kept him in good shape. He'd hate to think what he'd feel like if he were in bad shape. At the moment, his muscles felt like rubber.

He looked around the room at the other beds where men and women lay. Todd was in the next bed over. Roper was next to him.

Jesus! Was it Roper that had caused all the damn problems? What was it with the guy? He must have some information that Sterling wanted. But he was in no shape to survive if they tried to wake him up. So Sterling had sent Preston in there to ruthlessly pry it out of him. Had anyone found him? Or had he figured out a really good place to hide. Landon the designer of the VR might have some thoughts about that.

And hadn't Sterling said he was taking Lily and Hamilton to the guy? But where was that, exactly. Mack had no idea.

He looked toward the cabinets where rows of shelves held drugs. Probably there was a stimulant in there that would get him moving. Or it might kill him. Yeah, better stay away from stimulants for now.

Still fighting dizziness, he crossed the room, holding on to beds as he made his way to an open cabinet where he saw hospital scrub suits. There were more of them on the shelves, and he awkwardly exchanged his hospital gown for the pants and top, cursing his rubbery arms and legs. Then he looked around for the desk where Grant had stowed his gun.

Oh great, there were a couple of desks. Which one had his brother's weapon?

CHAPTER TWENTY-SIX

"Leave her alone," Grant shouted, hearing his own desperation as he looked at Jenny.

"Can't I give her one little jolt? Just for fun," the sadistic bastard asked.

"Please. Don't. I'll tell you anything you want to know," Grant answered, hating that he'd given in to this creep, yet knowing he couldn't be the cause of Jenny's pain.

Preston looked at him, a satisfied expression on his face. "Did you find Roper? Are your brother and Wardman helping him? And they sent you back here to distract me."

"No. None of that."

"Then where did Bradley and Wardman go?"

"Out of here."

"What do you mean?" The man looked from the control box in his hand to Jenny, then back again. "There's no way out of here. This VR is to give coma victims some kind of life."

"Lily's a physician. She's part of the medical team, with in and out access to this place through a portal in her room. They used it to go back to the lab."

"Oh yeah?

"Yeah."

"Then your brother's a dead man. Lily may be in normal physical shape, but Mack Bradley is not."

Grant spoke through clenched teeth. "She said his injury was a result of his twisting his neck. In the lab he opened his eyes and responded to me. He's got a chance."

Preston laughed. "You can think so, if it makes you feel better."

"Let me go."

"You say she has a machine in her room where she can communicate with the lab."

Grant nodded.

"Then let's go up there."

Suddenly the bonds that held Grant to the pillar disappeared, and he fought to keep his balance. When he was steady on his feet, he rushed across to Jenny, who was also freed. He reached for her, taking her in his arms and murmuring reassuring words to her as he zipped up her jacket over her torn shirt.

"You're okay. Everything's okay."

"Oh God. I thought this place was safe," she answered.

"It will be," he whispered.

"I hate to interrupt this tender scene, but let's go," Preston said. "Show me where to find her room."

Mack fought the sick feeling in his throat as he moved from one desk to the next, opening drawers. The gun was in the third place he looked, and he breathed a sigh of relief as he closed his hand around the butt, then checked to make sure the weapon was loaded.

Okay, now he was armed. The next step was to figure out where Sterling had taken Lily and Hamilton.

He was about to leave the room when another thought occurred to him. He'd come here because a hacker named Preston was wreaking havoc in the VR. Maybe it would be a good idea to keep him from finding out what was going on over here.

The communications equipment was on one of the desks where Mack had looked for the gun. He staggered back there and stood for a moment studying the setup. When he couldn't figure out how to turn it off, he pulled a bunch of plugs from the power strip, hoping he hadn't destroyed anything important in the process.

Or maybe he'd acted too fast. Maybe he would have found a directory of the building in the computer—if he'd even known where to look for it.

He stood for a moment, holding on to the desk, swaying on his feet, cursing himself for not getting his butt in gear.

And then another thought skittered into his mind.

Call Decorah Security.

Had he come up with that on his own? He didn't think so, but it was what Grant had told Lily if she needed help.

That was as true now as it had been back in the VR. She needed help, and so did he.

He was torn. He wanted to dash down the hall and find Lily, but he didn't know where she was. And if he fell over in a dead faint, that wasn't going to do her any good.

Grant had told Lily the Decorah number, but Mack's numb brain couldn't dredge it up. In the end, he had to go through information.

The phone was picked up on the first ring by a guy with a crisp voice.

"This is Mack Bradley, Grant Bradley's brother. He told me to call if I needed help."

"Just a moment."

He waited for agonizing seconds before another voice came on the line. "This is Frank Decorah. What can I do for you?"

"Did Grant tell you I'd been killed ... in the Middle East?"

"Yes."

"I was taken captive. It's a long story. I'm at a lab in Gaithersburg. Hamilton Labs. I was being held in a virtual reality experiment."

"Wait. Slow down."

"I was in a coma. A bunch of us in similar conditions woke up in a virtual reality. Like being in a video game, only more real. I'm out—but weak. Grant went in because it's

196

under attack by a hacker, and he's still there. Dr. Hamilton's financial backer, a guy named Sterling, has taken him and Dr. Lily Wardman captive in the Hamilton building—but I don't know where. I'm in the lab with the sleepers." He dragged in a breath and let it out. "This probably sounds crazy."

"No. We're on our way. Do you know where Sterling was taking them?"

"He said to Sidney Landon, the program designer, but I don't even know where that is."

He heard keys clicking in the background.

"Second floor. Room 289."

"Jesus. How do you know?"

"One of my computer guys called up the building specs while we were talking."

"Okay." He stopped. "And if I'm in the lab with the patients who are in comas, where am I?"

"Third floor. You're in the back of the building. Room 389 is in the front.

"I'm going down there."

"Wait for some of my men."

"I can't." He stopped, trying to clear his head. "Be careful. Sterling has trained killers working for him. They tricked Grant into meeting them at the FDR Memorial, then tried to kill him."

"Christ. I wish I'd known about that sooner. Stay on the line with me. We're en route now."

"I can't. I don't have a portable, and this landline is in the medical ward with the patients."

"Stay where you are."

"I can't," he repeated, fear for Lily rising like a tidal wave threatening to drown him.

He'd already taken too much time talking to Decorah. Slamming down the receiver, he turned to the cabinet where the drugs were kept and started looking at labels. Thank God there were several stimulants on the shelves, probably because a patient who woke up might need them.

Like him. Lily had given him a shot of something. Was it okay to take another hit, too?"

Fuck it!

He swallowed a capsule without water, praying that it would kick in soon—and wouldn't make him feel like he was bouncing off the ceiling. If he'd dared, he would have taken two, but he knew that was plain stupid.

Teeth gritted he started down the hall, moving cautiously, on the lookout for the men who had tried to kill Grant.

There were none of the invaders on this floor, but he found a guy in a scrub suit. Maybe an orderly who had been working with the patients. He'd been shot through the head and chest and was lying on the floor of a small office.

Christ! The poor guy.

Seeing there was nothing he could do, Mack backed away.

By the time he reached the stairs, he was feeling steadier on his feet and was thinking more clearly, unless he was fooling himself on that point.

Cautiously he opened the stairwell door and looked up and down. He saw no guards. Probably Sterling thought everyone else in the building was a zombie.

He made it to the second floor, then slowly opened the door. Still no guards.

Had Sterling dismissed them? Or perhaps he had sent them down in case someone tried to enter the building. Which was too bad for the Decorah guys.

He should have asked how many were coming. But he'd been too focused on getting to Lily—because he was in love with her.

Love? The idea was crazy. He hadn't known her long enough, yet he knew it was true. And he knew she'd only been doing her job in the VR. Their relationship might have started off with her lying to him and everybody else who was part of the experiment, but what choice had she had?

He looked at the room number nearest him. 330. 389 must be down the hall and maybe around the corner.

He moved cautiously, his weapon at the ready as he paused by each doorway and listened.

As he approached the cross hallway, he heard footsteps coming toward him from the left. He ducked into the nearest room, holding the door open just a crack as he saw two men round the corner.

"I don't know why he's having us patrol," one of them said. Was it one of the guys Grant had encountered at the memorial?

"Yeah, nobody here but zombies."

The other guy laughed as they passed. Mack watched their backs as they moved away.

Now he was between them and the room where Sterling was holding Lily and the others. If he went down the hall and they turned around, they could shoot him in the back.

Shit!

Overhead he thought he heard the whir of a helo, then it kept going, and he figured it was one of the patrols that had routinely flown over the DC area since 9/11.

He looked down the hall again, seeing one of the men pull open the door to the stairway. If they were going down, that would get them out of the way—unless they noticed that one of the patient beds was now empty and an IV line was dripping on the floor.

How many more men were patrolling the building? And where were they exactly? Probably some of them were with Sterling to help keep his captives under control.

Mack started down the hall again. He wanted to run, but he couldn't take the chance of being spotted—or on using up his limited supply of energy.

He rounded the corner and moved a few doors down, until he realized from the numbers that he was going the wrong way.

Cursing, he reversed directions, forcing himself to stop and look for more guards where the hallways intersected. When he saw none, he sprinted across, then headed for room 289

Before he had taken more than a dozen steps, the sound of automatic gunfire sounded from the floor below.

CHAPTER TWENTY-SEVEN

What the hell?

Mack ducked back around the corner as two men ran out of the office and headed toward the set of stairs at the other end of the hall. As he heard them pounding down the steps, he moved quickly toward his goal. Mack knew the gunfire downstairs would have put Sterling on alert. But he couldn't simply stay in the hall. Gun in hand, he slid around the doorjamb just far enough to see partway into the room.

Sterling was also holding a gun, but looking in the direction where his men had gone. He was half turned away from Mack and had completely turned his back on the captives as more gunfire rattled up from downstairs.

When Lily looked up and spotted Mack in the doorway, he saw her eyes widen. Relief flooded her features, but she mouthed,

"Wait."

His heart was in his throat as he watched her edging toward the desk. In one quick motion, she picked up a decorative paperweight, and lunge toward Sterling, slamming the glass ball down onto their captor's head.

As the man went down, Mack leaped into the room, took the gun and handed it to Landon.

Lily reached for him, and he pulled her into his arms, just for a moment.

"Are you all right?" they both asked.

"Yes."

She drew back and gave him a considering look. "I saw you open your eyes, but I thought you couldn't get up."

"When that bastard took you, I knew I couldn't just lie there."

"What's happening?" she asked as the sound of more gunfire reached the second floor. "Who's down there?"

"I called Decorah Security, like Grant said. If it's them, I can't believe they got here that fast."

She nodded.

They heard footsteps on the stairs, this time coming up, and Mack turned toward the door, his weapon at the ready.

"Mack Bradley," someone called out.

"Who wants to know?"

"This is Cole Marshall with Decorah Security."

"How do I know?"

"Fair point. Because I'm not shooting."

"How did you get here so fast?" Mack challenged.

"Helicopter."

"Come out where we can see you."

A tall, dark-haired man stepped into view and held up his hands.

They heard more footsteps coming up, and it sounded like someone who had a slight limp. An older man with dark hair, now shot through with gray, stepped out and looked toward Mack.

"I'd say you were Grant if I didn't know he had a twin brother," he said.

"You're Frank Decorah?"

"Right."

"What happened downstairs?"

"When we came across the parking lot, some men started shooting. We had no choice but to defend ourselves."

"They're dead?"

"Yes," Decorah answered.

"How many?"

"Five."

"And we've got two more men besides me and Cole," the agency owner said.

Mack had heard about him from Grant and knew he was an ex-Navy SEAL, who'd lost most of a leg in Vietnam. He was a mysterious figure who kept strictly to himself when he was away from the office, yet Grant suspected that he had a secret life he shared with no one.

"You said your brother is in the VR?" Decorah asked.

"Yes. I don't know what happened there after I left. I just know that Sterling came in here and grabbed Lily."

"Have you and Grant used your talent to communicate?"

Mack was surprised at the casual way Frank Decorah referred to his and his twin's ability to send silent messages to each other.

"A little," Mack said. "We lost it in our teens, but it seems to have come back."

"A crisis brings out psychic abilities. And once you've got a handle on it, you can be trained to do more."

Mack wanted to think about that, but he didn't have that luxury now.

He motioned for them to step into the office. Lily was holding Sterling's own gun on him as he sat on the floor, groaning and gingerly touching his head. Hamilton and Landon were in back of her, both looking shell-shocked.

The man on the floor raised his head as Marshall and Decorah entered, obviously surprised to see someone new had appeared on the scene.

"Who the hell are you? Where are my men?"

"Your men fired on us," Frank Decorah answered in a steely voice. "We gave them a chance to surrender, but they declined." He raised one shoulder. "They lost the fight."

"Jesus. No," Sterling answered.

Mack turned toward him, wondering if he was sorry his men were dead or sorry that he was now unprotected. "I think it's time to tell us what the hell is going on." For the newcomers' benefit, he added some background. "Dr.

Hamilton was running an experimental project for patients in a coma. He put them into a virtual reality where they could function as though they were awake." He gestured toward the designer. "Sidney Landon is the genius programmer who created the virtual world."

Landon flushed.

"But a guy named Preston hacked in and created a bunch of fantasy effects, like large animals and small but vicious warriors. It appears he was hired by Sterling to contact one of the patients—George Roper."

Sterling raised his head. "I didn't hire anyone to hack in."

"Oh come on," Mack responded. "If you didn't, who did?"

Sterling looked sick, but he shook his head. None of this was making perfect sense, but Mack pressed on because Sterling was his only link to the hacker in the VR.

"At least you can tell us what's so special about Roper."

The man on the floor turned his head to the side.

Mack hauled him to his feet and shoved him into one of the rolling desk chairs. Then he rummaged in the desk drawers until he found packing tape which he used to secure the captive, taping his arms to the chair arms and his legs to the metal legs.

Turning to the program designer, he asked, "Can you get a window into the VR?"

"Yes."

"Okay. Let me get this bastard out of view."

Mack wheeled Sterling's chair into the hall, then turned to the others. "It's better if Frank and Cole are out of sight, too. And also Lily." Looking directly at her, he said, "If Preston asks, I'm going to tell him you're wounded and downstairs."

She nodded

"And I don't want to give him and Sterling a chance to communicate."

Again she agreed.

Leaving everyone else in the hall, he returned to the designer's office and said, "Okay, go ahead and get me in there—I mean visually."

As Landon tapped on some keys, a picture of the matching computer in Lily's closet flashed onto the screen, and Mack gasped when he saw what was going on.

Grant and Jenny were standing in front of the monitor looking grim-faced, and Preston was standing right behind them, smiling.

"I was hoping you'd join us," he said, then gave Mack an assessing look. "I see you're not dead."

"I'm fine."

"I doubt it."

"What do you want?"

"You know what I want. George Roper."

"He's not here," Mack answered. "At least his mind isn't."

Preston's gaze flicked to Landon. "But I think you can find him in the VR. If you change the mode, you should have a blip on your screen for everyone in the VR. Like the CIA with their tracking devices."

"Is that true?" Mack asked.

"If I set it up that way. But it wasn't anything I needed to do. I have to figure it out."

"You'd better, or I'm going to kill these two." He gestured toward Grant and Jenny. First one and then the other."

He glanced at his two captives. "Double torture for Grant. I think he's going to hate watching Jenny die, so I'll do her first."

"You touch them, and I'll fucking kill you," Mack spat out.

"And how are you going to do that?" the man who was only a virtual copy of himself asked.

"I'll think of something."

As Landon bent over the computer keyboard, Mack stepped back into the hall and motioned to Lily. When she was beside him, he brought his mouth to her ear and spoke in a whisper, "You've got to bring everyone back from the VR, where he can't touch them."

She gave him a desperate look.

"You think it won't work?" he asked.

"I hope it will."

Before she could say more, Preston called from the VR, "Hey, where are you going?"

He stuck his head back into the office. "To clean up a mess we have here. Guys shot their way into the building, and Dr. Wardman was wounded. You don't want the cops to find the assault team, do you?"

There was a moment's hesitation before Preston said, "No."

Mack returned to the hall where Lily's anxious look brightened a little when she saw him again.

"My brother and Jenny are in the most danger. Do them first," he told her. "Then the others."

"But none of them can wake up."

"That's okay. They can stay asleep. Just bring Grant around."

Mack swung toward Hamilton.

"You're going to help Lily."

"But the experiment will be screwed up."

Mack fixed him with a look that was deadly enough to kill. "For Christ's sake. You think the experiment is worth shit now? Just do it. And plug the computer in the lab back in. I disabled it, but we may need it now."

Hamilton muttered a curse.

Mack longed to pull Lily into his arms and hold her, but there was no time for anything personal between them now. They had to finish this business before there could be any time to figure out where their relationship was going.

He turned to Decorah and Marshall. "I'd feel better if you go with them, just in case there are still bad guys hiding somewhere."

"Good point," Decorah answered.

Mack watched the four of them disappear into the stairwell, then turned back toward Landon's office.

He was about to step inside when Sterling raised his voice as he shouted, "Preston. Do you hear me, Preston?"

While he tried to say more, Mack leaped toward him and clamped his hand over the man's mouth as he raced his chair down the hall and away from the designer's office.

When they'd rounded the corner, he took his hand away from the man's mouth and slapped him soundly across the face. It was hard to keep himself from slamming his fist into the bastard's face again and again. But there was no time for that kind of personal satisfaction, either.

"What the hell do you think you're doing?" Mack bellowed.

Sterling raised his gaze defiantly. "I'm not going to just let you fuck everything up."

"What?" Mack raged. "You've already lost."

"And you're not going to get what you want either."

Mack didn't answer. He was thinking Lily was lucky this guy hadn't killed her when he'd taken her out of the lab at gunpoint. But probably he figured he needed her to make sure Roper stayed alive. And then what?

Mack fought the impulse to simply pull out his gun and shoot the man right now. But he knew that saving him for questioning would be prudent.

"I'll see you later," he said as he tore off strips of packing tape for a gag. Then he pushed the chair into a nearby office and made sure the captive's bonds were tight before turning back to Landon's office.

As he walked through the door, he felt like he'd walked into a scene from a horror movie—but what he was watching on the screen was no fantasy.

Preston was now holding Grant, a knife pressed to his throat.

"What the hell is going on?" Preston demanded. "How long is this going to take?"

Until all the people are out of the VR, Mack sent the message toward his brother. *And you're first.*

Jenny's first.

Landon turned and gave Mack a wide-eyed look.

Aloud he said, "We're mopping up after the invasion and making sure all the patients are okay." Mack looked at Landon. "Have you located Roper?"

"Yes."

Preston's expression turned feral. "Where is he?"

Landon looked at Mack, who kept his gaze fixed on the screen.

"Let go of my brother."

"Give me the information first."

Hoping he'd wasted enough of Preston's time, Mack turned to Landon and nodded. "Go ahead."

"He's down in the service area of the hotel. There's a doorway that I had blocked up. Apparently he found a way to pull some boards away."

Preston gave a satisfied smirk, until Grant suddenly vanished from his grasp.

He looked around in confusion like he'd been holding the nuclear football, and it had evaporated. "What the hell?" he shouted as he reached for Jenny.

She gasped, looking for Grant. But just as Preston's hand closed around her arm, she also disappeared.

"Fuck!" the hacker called as he turned and raced out of the bedroom and into the hallway.

"He's going for the others," Mack shouted.

"On it," Landon answered. The scene switched to the hallway, where a bunch of furniture from the bedrooms—sofas, chairs and tables had suddenly blocked the corridor.

Preston screamed as he tore at them, throwing them out of the way.

"He's so mad, he's forgotten that he can just hack them away," Landon said in satisfaction, piling up more debris as fast as Preston threw it out of the way.

"Keep going," Mack shouted over his shoulder. He was already out of the room and racing for the stairs, his heart pounding and his breath sawing in and out of his lungs.

He made it to the next floor, then had to lean against the wall while he caught his breath, silently cursing that he wasn't in better shape.

Mack brought Sterling down in the elevator and stashed him in a nearby room. When he arrived in the lab, followed by the Decorah men, Grant was already sitting up in his bed, looking like he couldn't believe he was back in the real world after his stint in captivity.

Lily and Hamilton were bending over two of the other patients.

"How many left?" Mack asked.

"Just Todd and Rendell."

"Is she okay after what he did to her?"

"Her blood pressure is a little high, but I think she's going to make it," Lily answered.

"And you've got Roper?" Mack clarified.

"Yes," Hamilton answered.

Mack turned back to the screen. "Shut the VR down," he told Landon.

"But Preston will be trapped without—anything. No air. No light. No sensation.

"That's the idea."

As Landon turned back to his keyboard, Grant climbed down from his bed and went to Jenny. Leaning over her, he spoke softly.

Mack felt his heart squeeze as he watched his brother try to communicate with the unconscious patient. Grant had found a woman he cared about, and she was stuck in a make-believe world. Or was there hope for her—the way there had been hope for him?

Maybe later, Mack thought as he watched Landon turn back to his keyboard.

. . .

Danny Preston gasped, or he would have gasped if there had been air to breathe.

A moment ago he'd been madly throwing furniture out of his way so that he could get to the location where Landon had found Roper. Now he was nowhere.

Terror tightened his chest. He tried to calm himself. He didn't have to breathe in here. This was only a virtual world, and his body was safe in an office building near Hamilton Labs.

But he couldn't stop the panic sensations from threatening to swallow him like a whale that had opened its mouth to suck in little fish.

Ineffective curses chased themselves through his mind. He'd never thought of himself as a sadist, but he'd been desperate enough to torture people in the VR while he searched for Roper. Now that bastard at the keyboard back in the lab had turned the tables on him. Worse than turned the tables because he was nowhere. Nothing.

He tried to move his hand. Tried to bring it to his face so he could at least feel something, but he couldn't even lift his arm. No. He had no arm. No body. No touchstone to reality. And he knew that time was short before he went bonkers—or died trying to drag imaginary air into his lungs.

Stay calm, he warned himself. *There's nothing you can do except wait for them to turn this place on again.*

But who was that going to be?

Did "Mr. Smith," the man who'd come to him with the deal of a lifetime, even have a clue what was happening now?

No way of knowing.

Danny could only pray that someone found him soon.

Pray? He couldn't remember the last time he'd done it, but now he couldn't help thinking it was his only hope.

Mack had just allowed himself to relax a fraction when two men he'd never seen before stepped into the lab, guns drawn.

One looked like he was in his thirties, with the eager expression of a novice on an exciting mission. The other was older, with more of a "seen it all" air.

"Nobody move. Hands in the air," the older one said.

Jesus, now what?

As everyone in the room turned toward the speaker, Mack tried to assess his chances of getting to the weapon he'd laid on the desk.

CHAPTER TWENTY-EIGHT

Mack decided he'd only get himself shot if he went for the gun. But what the hell was going on, exactly? Had more of Sterling's men shown up in time to seek revenge for their comrades' deaths?

"I said hands in the air, and turn this way," the older man ordered.

Everyone in the lab complied. The guy in charge spoke again,

"I'd like to know why there are a bunch of dead bodies piled up around the entrance to this building," he said in a surprisingly even voice, given the circumstances.

As he studied the group, he zeroed in on Decorah.

"Frank?"

"Marty?"

The two men stared at each other as though they had both stumbled into a crack house by mistake.

Frank Decorah turned to Mack. "Marty Weld and I were in rehab together at the Naval Medical Center, mumble mumble years ago, after we were both injured in Vietnam. I went into the security business. He joined the FBI and became a Special Agent."

The man and his younger associate were still holding their guns, but they looked a lot more friendly than they had when they'd come up here to find out about the gun battle.

"What are you doing here?" Weld asked Frank.

"I was called in because the building was under siege—from men working for a guy named Avery Sterling."

"We know about him," Weld clipped out.

"His men fired on my guys, and we won."

"Where is he?"

"I tied him up and put him in an empty office," Mack said.

Weld nodded and lowered his gun, then inclined his head toward his younger colleague. "This is Gordinger."

"Nice to meet you. I'm Mack Bradley," Mack said.

"And you are involved how?"

"I was one of the patients in Dr. Hamilton's experiment. I take it that, if you know about Sterling, you know what this lab is doing?"

"Yeah," Weld answered without giving anything away.

Everybody in the room gave their names and explained their role.

When they were finished, the agent in charge said, "Take us to Sterling."

Mack led the way to the room where he'd left the thug. The man was slumped in the chair. When he saw he had visitors, he sat up straighter and glared at them.

"Take him out to the van," Weld said to his associate.

"Right."

"Get the hell away from me," Sterling shouted when the younger man bent to untie him."

Weld assessed the situation. "Maybe we're better off leaving him tied and wheeling him out,"

"No! Wait."

"You have something to tell us?"

"Who are you?"

"FBI."

Sterling blanched.

Weld jerked his hand toward the door, and Gordinger wheeled the chair toward the elevator.

They all returned to the lab where Hamilton and Lily were attending to the patients.

"Maybe he'll talk when you get him downtown."

"Maybe," Weld said.

"Why did he stash Roper in the VR, then hire Preston to question him?" Grant asked.

Weld tipped his head to the side. "You got the first part right. Sterling stashed him here. With the cooperation of Doctor Hamilton."

They all looked at the doctor.

"Sterling was keeping the project funded," Hamilton bit out. "And he got me some additional patients. I don't see anything wrong with that."

"You mean like me?" Mack asked.

Blood drained from Hamilton's face.

The agent jumped back into the conversation. "But Sterling didn't hire Preston."

"What?" Mack swung toward him, wondering if he'd heard that right. He'd figured out the only way this whole thing could make sense. Now Weld was telling him something different?

"You're right about Sterling stashing Roper here—hoping he'd wake up," the FBI agent said. "But Preston's not working for Sterling. He's working for me."

"Huh?" Mack asked.

"I hired him, under the alias of 'Mr. Smith.' I sent him in there to find out which of the patients Sterling had brought here. And he did it. He called a little while ago and gave me Roper's name."

Grant looked as dumbfounded as Mack felt. "You mind explaining that?" he asked.

"Preston was in the pen for hacking into a couple of major banks. We sprang him so he could be in contact with the VR," Weld said.

"But why?" Mack asked.

"To be succinct, Sterling's got a lot of business interests. One of them is chemical manufacturing. He lost a lucrative chemical weapons contract that he probably should have been awarded. But there was some kind of under-the-table stuff going on at DOD. Sterling was boiling mad about it and decided to get the money he'd lost out of the government in a different way. He hired someone to place bombs loaded with toxic chemicals in subway systems in major cities."

Hamilton shook his head in denial. "No."

"Yes."

"What do you mean bombs with toxic chemicals?" the doctor demanded.

"Just what it sounds like. Bombs that are going to kill a lot of people. There are different timers at different locations. And if they go off, people riding the systems will breathe the stuff and die. We've kept it quiet to prevent mass hysteria, because we can't shut down every subway system in the country. Sterling was planning to blackmail the U.S. government, but we think his agent got cold feet after he planted the devices."

The man kept speaking. "We were trying to find out exactly who it was when he disappeared. Our best guess is that Sterling's men were closing in on him, and he had an accident while he was trying to go into hiding. Sterling's guys got to him before we could, spirited him away, and arranged to have him brought here. We've been beating the bushes for him. Then we picked up communications between Sterling and Hamilton and zeroed in on the lab."

"You can't find the bombs? Can't Sterling tell you where they are?"

"He didn't want to know. We found one in Boston and disabled it with minutes to spare. Do you know how many subway systems there are in the U.S. and how many places there are to hide an explosive device?"

"You have a point."

"So we hired Preston to get the information out of the guy who planted the bombs."

"From what I've seen, it looks like Preston's brilliant," Mack said. "Unfortunately, he's also out of control. He's threatening to kill people in the VR if he didn't get Roper."

"He's an outstanding hacker," Weld agreed. "He was serving fifteen to twenty years for the bank heists, and we got him out for this job. We told him that if he didn't complete it, he was going back. That's why he's willing to use any method available to locate Roper and pry the information out of him. Sorry if he went over the top."

"Just great," Mack muttered as he realized they were in trouble.

He rushed toward the computer screen and shouted at Landon who was sitting in his office. "You already shut down the VR with Preston in there?"

"Right."

The agent swore and looked toward Hamilton. "What does that mean? What happens to Preston now?"

"He's got no air in there. No senses. He could die or go crazy," the researcher answered in a flat voice.

"But it's just a virtual world, isn't it?" Weld asked, sounding like a man who had thought he was safe at the edge of a cliff and now felt the world crumbling out from under him.

"That doesn't prevent it from having real effects," Lily answered. "That's why the crap Preston was pulling on the patients worked."

Mack was madly revising his plans as Weld looked at Frank Decorah and Cole Marshall.

The FBI agent spoke to the private security men. "We appreciate the help you've given us, but I think it would be better if you leave."

Decorah looked reluctant, and finally inclined his head toward Grant. "Walk with me."

Grant followed him out of the room, then came back alone, giving Mack a long look.

Bad idea to send him away.

Yeah. But we'll waste time challenging the FBI. Unfortunately.

Mack took a quick breath. He had the feeling there was more Grant wanted to say, but there wasn't time to focus on that now.

Instead, he turned back to Weld. "We have to go in and get Preston."

"You can go in and out of there?"

"Yes." He swung back toward the screen where they could see Landon up in his office. "You're going to have to bring the VR back up again."

"I just shut it down."

"Yeah, but the situation has changed. We need Preston to help us now. I'm going in to get him. Where is he?"

"I left him in the upper hall near Lily's room, next to the pile of furniture I was using to keep him from getting downstairs and attacking the others"

"Can you send me there?"

"Yes. Since I sent your brother in, I've been changing the parameters so I can use any location for an entry point."

"If you revive Preston," he's going to be mad as hell. He's a pretty volatile guy," Weld said.

"Yeah, we noticed. But do you have a better idea?"

The agent shook his head.

"Okay. When I find Preston, am I authorized to tell him that he fulfilled his agreement with you?"

"Maybe he hasn't."

"Listen, you want him to cooperate, right?"

"Yeah."

"Then we have to give him what he wants."

The agent nodded, and Mack wasn't sure what Weld was agreeing to. Did he mean the accord could be a sham? Or was he willing to release Preston when this was over?

There was no time to argue about any of that now. Mack had to get in there—fast.

He looked toward the bed where he'd been confined earlier. "No reason to pretend I'm a patient. I can just wear my street clothes. That will save time."

"What do you mean 'I'? I'm going with you," Lily said.

"It's too dangerous," he answered immediately.

"You're not going without me," she said, punching out the words. "And if Preston needs medical attention, you'll need me."

Mack hesitated, but if bombs with deadly chemicals could go off at any moment, he wasn't about to waste time arguing, and Lily was already climbing onto the bed that she'd used earlier.

He kicked off his shoes and lay down. As Hamilton strode toward him, his eyes met the doctor's.

If he wanted, Hamilton could kill him now. Maybe he thought he had reason to do it.

Oops, something happened, and Bradley bought the farm.

Or maybe going back so soon was a bad idea.

He looked up to see that Grant was standing in back of the doctor.

"Take care of my brother if you want to stay healthy," he said in a low but gritty voice. The words sounded more like a warning than a request.

Hamilton gave him a startled look, then nodded as he began setting up the equipment for Mack.

"Ready?" the doctor asked.

"I'd better be."

He felt a prick in his arm.

"Count backwards from one hundred," the doctor said.

Mack started counting but didn't get any farther than ninety-seven.

He had the familiar sensation of being nowhere, and then he was back in the hotel, wearing the familiar running suit and tee shirt. He was lying on the rug in the hallway next to the pile of furniture that Landon said he had thrown into the corridor to keep Preston from getting to the people in the lobby.

Mack looked wildly around for Lily, and when he didn't see her, panic rose like a tsunami wave sweeping toward a ravaged shore.

Christ, had something happened to her in the transition?

Then he reminded himself that Hamilton couldn't send them both back at once. He'd started with Mack, and now he was doing the other fool who'd wanted to come back here. Still his heart pounded like a jungle telegraph gone wild until he saw her wink into existence on the carpet nearby.

"Thank God," he gasped, kneeling beside her.

He wanted to hold on to her and celebrate their crossing of a barrier that normal people never encountered, but there was no time for celebration now. Preston had been trapped in here without oxygen, and they had to focus on saving the man's miserable life.

Mack eyed the pile of furniture Landon had desperately thrown here. What a freaking mess.

"Shit, it looks like we landed on the wrong side." Taking a deep breath, Mack started reaching for furniture and tossing it out of the way.

With Lily working beside him, they began clearing a narrow path. When Mack ducked under a sofa that started to fall on him, Lily grabbed it, and they pushed it aside.

Several times they had to stop and prevent minor avalanches, but they finally made it to the other side of the heap. A few yards down the hall, they could see Preston lying on the carpet with his eyes closed.

Mack sprinted toward him, thankful that he was in a lot better shape in this virtual environment than he had been in the lab. Lily was right behind him. She felt for a pulse in Preston's neck, then breathed out what looked like a sigh of relief.

"Is he okay?" Mack asked anxiously.

"I hope so."

Mack was still leaning over the man when his eyes snapped open, and he focused on the people hovering over him.

"You bastards," he spat out. With surprising speed, his arm snapped up and pulled Mack down, grabbing him around the throat.

CHAPTER TWENTY-NINE

As steely fingers dug into his flesh, Mack dimly heard Lily scream. But her voice was in the background as he struggled to suck air into his lungs. The grip on his neck tightened, and he saw black dots dancing in front of his eyes.

Desperate to get Preston's hands off his throat, he bucked his body, and scrabbled at the man's fingers with his own, but it seemed that the hacker had no intention of letting go.

Mack fought the blackness closing in around him, feeling his strength draining away from the lack of oxygen. He tried to tell himself that none of this was real, but that had no validity as he felt the life being sucked out of him.

Then he heard a clunking sound, and suddenly the pressure on his neck was gone. Through dulled vision, he saw Lily grab Preston by the hair and roll him to his back, dropping him heavily on the floor.

"Wha.. ?" Mack tried to ask.

"Same technique I used in the lab. Only instead of a paperweight, I conked him with an *objet d'art,*" she said, gesturing toward the expensive-looking Oriental vase lying on the floor. "Are you okay?"

"I guess I'd better be. Thanks."

"I guess he figured a woman wasn't going to do anything dangerous."

"Helpful that he underestimated you."

The man was still out, but Mack knew that when he came to, he was going to be just as dangerous as when he'd attacked.

He didn't want to leave the hacker alone. If Roper could disappear in this place, so could Preston and gather his fantasy forces for another attack.

Picking up a leg that had come loose from a chair, Mack held it at the ready.

"Go down to your room and get Landon to send in a gun," he said. "Hurry."

Lily nodded, then ran down the hall to the room where Preston had held Grant and Jenny captive.

Mack divided his attention between the hallway and Preston. When Lily came back carrying an automatic pistol, Mack breathed out a little sigh. She handed him the weapon, and he checked the magazine.

Preston groaned. His eyelids fluttered. Then his eyes snapped open, and he focused on Mack.

"You bastards," he repeated what he'd said when he'd first spotted Mack and Lily.

"Take it easy."

"You tried to kill me."

"No, just put you out of commission—to keep you from hurting my brother and Jenny—or anyone else in here."

Preston snorted, then pushed himself up and gingerly fingered the lump on the back of his head.

"Your deal with the FBI is still on."

The man's eyes narrowed. "You know about that?"

"Yeah. An agent named Weld showed up at Hamilton's lab."

"He's Mr. Smith?"

"Yeah."

"Shit."

"No. It's good—for all of us. He told us about the chemical warfare bombs—and that you'd identified Roper."

"Uh huh"

"We don't know how much time we've got before the damn things go off. So let's get to it. How about we set up a scenario where Roper thinks there's no escape—unless he cooperates." When he explained what he had in mind, Preston laughed.

"I like the way your mind works."

"So you're in?"

"Yeah."

"You set up the room we'll need, and Landon can bring Roper back to the VR."

"I can do little stuff on the fly, but for something like this, I can't work with thin air. Can Landon send me a laptop?" the hacker asked.

"I don't see why not."

"A MacBook Pro."

The three of them went back to the bedroom and spoke to the VR designer. While they waited, Mack asked, "If Sterling is rich, why would he hatch a plot to kill thousands?"

"I think he didn't think it would happen. He'd get his money transferred to a Swiss bank, and everything would come out okay."

"But why risk it?"

"Apparently he was born with a silver spoon in his mouth. He always got everything he wanted, and when he fraudulently lost the contract, he was mad enough to shit bullets."

"What a sense of entitlement," Lily murmured.

"And what do you know about Roper?" Mack asked.

"Just what I skimmed off of his nasty little mind. He's a con man and a petty thug who was willing to take a dirty job for money."

The conversation halted when the laptop Preston had requested flashed into existence on the nearby dressing table.

The hacker sat down and started typing, and Mack started pacing back and forth, wondering if they were going to get the news of a chemical attack before they pried the information out of Roper.

After a few minutes, Mack saw a picture appear on the screen.

"Like this?" Preston asked without stopping what he was doing.

"Yeah. I like the stone walls."

"And we'll make it cold and damp." He looked over his shoulder at Mack and Lily. "Maybe you want to put on heavier jackets."

The bedroom vanished, and they were suddenly standing in the middle of what looked like a medieval dungeon with stone walls and only one high, barred window letting in a thin shaft of light. The air smelled musty and felt ten degrees lower than it had been. Torches burned in sconces. Manacles dangled from one wall, and various torture instruments decorated a nearby table.

"What do you think?" Preston asked with a note of pride in his voice. They couldn't see him, but they could hear him loud and clear.

"Perfect," Mack answered as Lily shuddered.

"Where are you?" Lily asked.

"Around the corner where he won't see me. It will seem like it's all coming from you."

Mack followed the hacker's voice and stepped around a section of the wall to a hidden alcove where Preston was sitting at a glass-topped table in an expensive modern office chair. The hacker had changed his clothing. He was now dressed like an old-time gunslinger in a leather duster, black cowboy hat and snakeskin boots.

He grinned and eyed Mack critically. "What was I thinking? Those running suits are much too tame for this performance."

Mack blinked as his own outfit changed. Now he was dressed like a medieval torturer, wearing tights, a tunic and a hood over his head with eyeholes that didn't obstruct his vision. High leather boots completed the outfit. And when Lily hurried around the corner, he saw she was similarly dressed—like a man.

Nice, a silent voice said in his head, and he knew his brother was commenting.

"What's this?" Lily demanded, waving her arm as she gestured toward the outfit.

"Women had no power back in those days," Preston explained.

"Thanks," she answered.

"We'd better get on with this," Weld called from the computer screen. He and the others were gathered in back of Landon.

As he studied Mack's costume, he asked, "Is this going to work?"

"You mean are we going to scare the shit out of Roper? I think so. He already suspected Preston was after him, which was why he hid in the hotel basement."

"You've got a point," the FBI agent conceded.

Mack addressed Preston. "One more thing I want. A brazier full of hot coals. With a poker sticking out."

"You got it."

A deep iron bucket with coals glowing in the bottom appeared in the corner. The long handle of a poker stuck out, topped with a blood-red hot pad to hold it.

"Thanks. Now send him in," Mack said. "I want him to wake up shackled to the wall."

"Naked?" Landon asked from the screen, obviously getting into the spirit of the drama that was about to unfold.

"No. We'll take care of that in here."

Lily gave him a startled look. "We'll do what?"

"Make him think he's going to be sorry if he doesn't talk." Mack added. "I know you're going to feel bad for him, but remember he was willing to kill a lot of people for money."

Mack motioned Lily back into the main chamber. When he turned toward the empty shackles, she followed suit, but more slowly.

"You can go back to the lab," he said.

"No. He might need a doctor."

"Yeah, he might."

Twenty seconds later, Roper flashed into view. His hands were circled by metal cuffs which pulled his arms up and fastened them to the wall. His feet were secured to metal chains that were cemented to the floor.

When he saw the two hooded figures, his head snapped up. He stared at them before his gaze flitted around the room.

When he tried to pull his hands away from the wall, the manacles and chains held him fast.

"Who are you? What's going on?" he demanded, but fear tinged his voice.

"You're here because you did a dirty little job for Avery Sterling."

Roper tipped his head to the side. "Wait a minute. I know that voice. You're the smart-ass Mack Bradley."

"If you say so."

Mack took a step forward, aware that Lily had cringed farther away from the man chained to the wall. He knew she didn't like this, but she wasn't going to run away from it, either.

"You're Bradley," Roper said again.

"Yeah, playing a new role."

"Let me out of here. You have no right to do this."

Mack ignored the assertion. "You caused a lot of grief in the VR."

Roper kept his face stony. "I had a right to protect myself."

"What's the last thing you remember?" Mack demanded.

Roper sighed. "Okay. Have it your way. I was in the hotel basement."

"Doing what?"

Roper started to answer, then pressed his lips together as he remembered why he'd been there.

When he didn't follow through, Mack did it for him. "Hiding from Preston."

"What do you mean? Everybody was trying to get away from Preston."

"Yeah, because he was trying to find *you*."

Roper shook his head, still putting up a good front.

"It's your fault all those innocent people were scared out of their minds."

"No."

"You know it's true. And you're going to find out that lying won't do you any good. We need to know where those bombs are, and you're going to tell us."

The man shook his head.

Mack looked at the implements laid out on the table and picked up a large pair of scissors. He held it up as he walked toward Roper.

"You were working for a guy named Sterling," he said. "Only you were afraid he was going to kill you when he finished with you. So you ran away."

Roper kept shaking his head, but he'd lost his bravado.

"The good news is that the FBI has him in custody. He can't hurt you now. It's safe to tell us where the bombs are."

"What bombs? I don't know about any bombs." Roper looked desperately around, but he still refused to give up the information they had to get.

Mack opened the guy's jacket and pushed it out of the way, then snapped the elastic of his waistband against his middle—hard.

Roper winced. Mack pulled the elastic away again so that he could insert one blade of the scissors between the fabric and Roper's body. Then he started cutting his way down the side of one pants leg.

The captive screamed. "What ... what are you doing?"

"Making a point." As Mack kept cutting, Roper started to struggle, trying to pull his hands free of the wall, then trying to kick out at Mack. But he was secured to the wall.

"Better stop moving around," Mack said in a dry voice, "Or I might cut something you don't want to lose."

Roper moaned.

Mack finished one leg, then turned to the other. "You're going to be naked from the waist down, in front of Lily Wardman." He inclined his head toward her. "But actually, she's a doctor, so she won't be seeing anything she hasn't seen a lot of times before."

"Get off me," Roper howled. "Get off me. Stop it."

Mack ignored him, cutting down the other leg until the sweatpants fell away and pooled around the man's feet.

Mack stepped back inspecting Roper's body and making a tsking sound.

Then he came forward again and inserted the blades in the fabric of the man's tee shirt, cutting partway up, then ripping the shirt the rest of the way.

"Are we ready to talk?" he asked.

"No. Leave me alone."

"You planted chemical warfare bombs in subways. They found one in Boston. What about the rest of them?"

The man shook his head violently. "I don't know about any bombs."

"Oh, right."

Mack studied the implements on the table, then shook his head. Instead he went to the brazier in the corner, wrapped the pot holder around the handle of the poker and picked it up. The end that had been in the coals was glowing red.

"I don't think this is going to feel too good," he said as he strode back to the man who was watching him with a horrified expression on his face.

"Don't. Oh God, please don't," he begged.

"Where are the bombs," Mack asked.

"I don't know."

"Like hell."

Mack could feel the heat radiating from the end of the poker. He held it up for Roper to see.

"Where should we burn you?" he asked in a conversational tone.

Behind him he could hear Lily draw in a strangled breath, but he forced himself to ignore how much she hated what they were doing to this man—even if he deserved worse.

Instead he moved toward the captive, holding out the poker, hoping he wasn't going to have to follow through on his threat.

"We can start with your thigh. If you don't talk, we can go on to your penis."

The hot iron was inches from Roper's thigh when he screamed, "No. Don't burn me. I'll tell you. I'll tell you."

Mack put the poker back into the fire. "Spill."

"You say they found the one in Boston?"

"Yeah. Where are the others?"

"I don't know."

"Don't give me that shit. You put them there."

"No."

Mack brought the tip of the poker close enough for Roper to feel the heat.

The man screamed. "No. Stop. I'll tell you."

Mack pulled the poker back when the world around them started flickering.

CHAPTER THIRTY

"Christ. What's going on?"

Fearing some kind of double cross, Mack ran around the corner to where Preston sat at the table. The look of surprise on the hacker's face told Mack that he hadn't been the cause of the disturbance, but he had to ask anyway. "Are you doing that?"

"Fuck, no."

"Then what?"

"Somebody's fooling with the electrical current in the lab. I think I can compensate, at least for a while."

Preston had brought up the lab on his screen. Mack swore as he saw the lights in the building had dimmed. Behind Landon, he saw Grant step through the doorway and wondered where he had gone.

Where were you? Mack asked.

Taking care of some business.

Mack's attention shifted to Hamilton, who was looking panicked. He picked up the phone and was speaking. Mack couldn't hear the conversation, but it was apparent that the line was dead.

"What's happened to the sound?" he asked Preston.

"It's off."

"Get it back."

"If I can," the hacker answered, frantically tapping on the keyboard.

As he watched the screen, he could see Grant look toward the exit, maybe calculating his chances of getting out of the lab before whoever was messing with the electronics in the building showed up.

I think I can tell you where the bombs are, Mack shouted in his mind, praying he could reach his brother.

He repeated the message, and at first nothing happened. Finally Grant stopped and looked toward the screen, an inquisitive expression on his face.

Give me a minute, Mack said.

I hope we've got a minute.

Rounding the corner again, Mack faced Roper, still trying to keep the connection with his brother as he spoke. "Tell me where to find those damn bombs."

"A lot of good it's going to do you now. Something's going on out there."

"Just fucking tell me." For emphasis he picked up the poker again and walked toward Roper. "Now."

The man gasped out, "One's in Baltimore, and two are in DC."

"That's not enough information. Where, exactly?"

"In DC, one's at Farragut North. One's at Silver Spring. In Baltimore, it's at the Lexington Market stop."

"You've got to do better than that," Mack shouted.

"I can't tell you from *here.* I need a map."

"Christ, we need to get the people out of those stations."

"How?" Lily asked desperately.

Grant? Mack shouted in his mind. *Grant, did you hear that?*

To his relief, his brother answered. *Yes.*

Thank God. Get the information to the FBI.

On it.

But before Grant could leave, more people stepped into view on Preston's screen.

One of them was Avery Sterling, a satisfied smirk on his face as he looked around the lab. Two of his men were with him. He turned toward Hamilton, who cringed away.

"How did he get loose?" Lily gasped.

"I wish I knew. The FBI was supposed to have him," Mack answered.

The man was shouting at Hamilton, clearly furious, and Mack fought the sick feeling that threatened to choke off his breath. Every time he thought a crisis was almost under control, another monster popped up.

Grant went stock-still as he stared at the men who had entered the lab.

Sterling's gaze swung toward him.

"Got ya."

Grant answered with a small nod.

The thug stepped toward the screen and pointed a gun at Landon. "I want to see what's going on in the VR."

Landon nodded. With a shaky hand, he pressed a button, and Sterling grinned as he looked directly at the trio gathered around the laptop. "That's it?"

"Yes," Landon answered.

"All I see is some kind of alcove, like the basement of a castle."

Landon shrugged. "Preston must have done that."

"Where's Roper?" he shouted at the three people he could see.

"They can't hear you," Grant answered.

"I wasn't talking to you. Shut up."

Grant closed his mouth, then saw the image on the screen change. Mack, Lily and Preston were replaced with the devil mask Preston had worn when he'd attacked Mack and Grant.

"Is that you, Preston, the guy everyone thought I hired?" Sterling shouted.

Of course there was no answer.

"Why can't I hear anything?"

"You did something to the power," Grant said.

"I did not," Sterling bellowed, sounding outraged. He turned toward the screen. "They need to hear me. Hamilton told me he had a way to get the information out of Roper."

"You can't get to him," Landon said. "He's in the VR, and the connection's turned flaky."

"If he won't talk, I can cut off his life support from here. And Preston's," he added.

"Not Preston's," Landon answered.

"Why not?"

"He's not in the lab."

"Where is he?"

"At an FBI safe house, I assume. I don't know for sure."

He was answered with a string of curses.

Sterling's face was red with anger as he turned to Grant.

"This is all your fault. I had a perfectly good deal going. I had the doctor add Roper to his zombie unit so I could find out where he put those bombs. But you stuck your nose in where it didn't belong."

"I wanted to find my brother. You sent Roper off to plant bombs, and you didn't even know where they were?"

"He said he'd pick the best places. Then he backed out of our deal."

"What I don't get is—why did you want a chemical attack at subway stations?"

"Because I was cheated out of a big contract. I figured I could get the money anyway. Then Roper double crossed me."

Grant shrugged. "Why did you change your mind about the attacks?"

"It was a bluff. I was never going to kill all those people. The feds would have hunted me down like Bin Laden. I was going to fix it. And then you had to open that stupid coffin and start asking a shitload of questions."

"I had a right to know what happened to my brother."

"He was safe here, you jerk. And you should have been eliminated at the monument." Sterling raised his gun and shot at Grant, three bullets striking him. He staggered backwards and went down, disappearing from sight behind one of the beds.

Mack watched in horror, still unable to hear what was going on in the lab. Christ, Sterling had just shot his brother.

He looked at Lily. "Can we get back in there?"

She shook her head. "We could, but then what. We'd wake up in those beds, and he'd just shoot us."

"But we have to help Grant."

She gave him a sick look. "I don't think there's anything we can do. Sterling hit him in the chest."

Mack wanted to rage. He wanted to charge around the corner and smash his fists into Roper, who was the cause of this whole damn mess. But he couldn't move away from the screen as he watched the action in the lab.

As Mack continued to stare at the screen in horror, Sterling turned to Hamilton and pointed the gun at him.

Even without a sound, Mack could tell the doctor was pleading for his life.

Before the attacker could fire, a gray shape leaped through the doorway, taking him down. It was an animal that looked a lot like a wolf.

Mack gaped as another wolf flattened one of the gunmen. And he blinked as his brother climbed off the floor and came up behind the other thug, shoving a gun in his back. His arm was bloody, and Mack could see bullet holes in his shirt. The only explanation he could come up with was that Grant had been wearing a bulletproof vest.

Thank the Lord.

234

The wolves kept Sterling and his men in check while Grant grabbed their guns. He looked toward the screen and spoke silently.

Sorry, Mack. The last part was a scam to get Sterling's confession on video. We didn't have any proof of the plot, and we needed him to incriminate himself. And we needed you to focus on getting the locations of the bombs out of Roper. It was all going according to plan, until Sterling came back sooner than we expected.

CHAPTER THIRTY-ONE

Mack felt for a nearby stone wall and sagged against it. He wanted to throttle Grant for not letting him in on the scheme, but he understood why it had to be held as closely as possible.

He turned to Preston and Lily. "The part with Sterling and his men was a setup. They wanted him to incriminate himself."

The sound came on and Grant said, "And I texted the location of the bombs to the FBI. They already have the stations cleared. And teams are going in in hazmat suits to find the devices."

Lily blinked. "But the sound was off. How did you know the locations?"

"Mack told me."

She looked from one to the other of them, then focused on Mack. "I don't understand."

Mack looked at her. "I told you about me and Grant communicating mind to mind. We lost it when we were teenagers, but the recent ... stress has made the ability a lot stronger than it ever was."

She nodded, still looking like she could hardly believe what they were telling her.

A shout from the main part of the dungeon caught their attention. It was from Roper.

"Hey, what about me? You can't just leave me here."

"You're right." Mack looked at his brother. *Tell Hamilton to bring him back there until we can figure out what to do with him.*

Grant conveyed the message to the doctor, who nodded and moved toward one of the beds.

Weld faced the screen. "Good job."

"How did you work it—making Sterling think he'd escaped?"

"We knew two of his guys were still in the area. We let them 'rescue' him."

"Wasn't that taking a chance on your getting killed?"

"We worked it like we did with Grant. And they were in a hurry to leave, so they didn't stop to verify that we were dead."

"And the Decorah team stayed on scene?" Mack asked.

"Yes," Frank answered. "We didn't go far."

Preston cleared his throat. "And what about me?" he asked, his gaze fixed on the FBI agent.

Weld gave him a studied look, and Mack knew the hacker was holding his breath.

"You kept your end of the bargain. We'll stick with ours," the FBI agent said to Preston.

The hacker let out a whoop. "Thank you."

"No one else could have pulled that off. I mean getting Roper to talk."

"I needed Mack Bradley to make it work," Preston said and turned to Mack. "Sorry I was such a bastard."

"A talented bastard. Too bad you had to scare the shit out of us." He wasn't going to add that it was "all right."

"Hope we meet again under better circumstances," Preston said just before he flickered out of existence.

"I guess he's gone back to the safe house," Lily said.

Mack looked around the corner and saw that Roper had also vanished. Presumably, he was back in the lab where Sterling had put him, and there was no reason to let him enjoy the five-star amenities of the Mirador Hotel.

But what about the innocent people whom Hamilton had brought there?

Mack was still wondering about them when he was suddenly also in the lab, lying in his old bed, with Hamilton looking down at him.

"How are you?" the doctor asked.

"Hopefully, better than I was last time I was here." He sat up cautiously and was glad he wasn't feeling weak or dizzy.

A few beds away, Lily was also sitting up. Their eyes met, and he wanted to get up and go to her, but there was still a lot of stuff to take care of. "Later," he mouthed.

She nodded.

He climbed down and stood holding the side of the bed, hoping he didn't look too wobbly on his feet.

Two dark-haired men had walked into the lab and were talking with Frank Decorah and Grant. One was Cole Marshall, who had been there earlier with Decorah.

"This is Brand Marshall," Decorah said, introducing the other man. "Cole's cousin. They were part of the takedown team."

Mack hadn't seen any men—only wolves. His eyes widened as he considered the implications of what Frank had said. Grant had hinted that there were men with highly unusual skills working for Decorah Security. These two guys must be some of the most interesting.

Weld was speaking again—to Hamilton. "And you are under arrest."

The doctor blanched. "For what?"

"For stealing patients without permission. For cooperating in a scheme to blackmail the U.S. government."

"I didn't know about his scheme," Hamilton answered.

"You just thought you were making a sweet deal for funding?"

"Yes."

"Well, you should have remembered the old investment rule—if it seems too good to be true, it is."

Gordinger stepped forward and pulled out a pair of handcuffs, which he clamped onto the doctor.

"I want a lawyer," Hamilton shouted.

"Of course. And maybe you can cut a deal—like Preston."

When the doctor had been removed, Lily turned to Weld.

"But what about the program? I mean, those poor people." She swept her hand toward the sleeping patients.

Frank Decorah was the one who answered. "I think we can continue the program. Not for experimental purposes, but as a refuge for patients who could benefit." He cleared his throat. "After we establish that the other patients are here legitimately. Or if they were stolen like Mack, we'll inform the relatives."

"Yes," Lily agreed. "But who is going to run it?"

"You."

Her eyes widened. "But I was Hamilton's junior associate."

"You're perfectly capable of the technical aspects, and I suspect your ethics are a lot better than Hamilton's."

She looked stunned and at the same time excited. "Where would we go?"

"There's a vacant warehouse near my office. We could fit it out as a medical unit."

Lily looked overwhelmed that things were moving so fast. "That's going to take money. And I need some additional medical staff."

"Decorah has a foundation that can handle the costs," Frank said. He looked at Mack and Grant. "And I think two telepathic security men who have already been in the VR would be ideal for the project."

Mack shook his head. "I can't just leave the Navy—and go AWOL."

Frank laughed. "Why not? You're officially dead."

He hadn't thought of that.

"But I beat the bushes looking for him," Grant said.

"Does anyone know you found him?"

"Anyone official? No."

"Well, then. In fact, his being dead is a definite advantage. It gives him operating space you wouldn't otherwise have. He can make himself a whole new identity."

Mack's head was spinning as he tried to take it all in.

Beside him, Lily spoke. "Somehow Preston got my sister into the VR. Can I bring her back and give her a chance for life that she's never had since her accident?"

"Of course," Frank answered, then looked from Lily to Landon and back again. "Can you keep this place running while I contact some medical personnel I trust?"

"Yes."

"You can hire your own staff, of course. But I think you need some help now."

Lily looked at the patients. "It will be less complicated if we keep them here sleeping until the move is completed."

"Yes," Frank agreed. "If you think there's someone who's not suitable for the VR—either temperamentally or physically—they can be transferred somewhere else. I think Mack can help us rate their suitability."

"Yes," he agreed. "But I'd hate to exclude someone just because they're a little difficult to get along with."

Lily gave him a long look. "Right. But first, I want you to have a medical exam."

He looked startled. "I'm fine."

"You left the VR against your doctor's advice. I want to make sure you're okay."

He might have protested or said they'd have been in a hell of a mess if he hadn't returned to the real world, but he was starting to feel a little ragged around the edges, and he knew she was right. He'd better make sure he was fit for duty.

He went down the hall with Frank Decorah to a room that was set up as a lounge.

Like everything else Frank Decorah had arranged that day, the doctor arrived in record time. He gave Mack a thorough exam and made some recommendations—like his seeing a neurologist and having some physical therapy.

RX MISSING

"But right now, my best advice is to get some rest," he said.

As soon as the guy said it, Mack knew it was an excellent idea. He'd been up for hours, and the stimulant he'd taken had long since worn off.

He kicked off his shoes and flopped onto the couch. As he settled down, he figured he had time for a short rest. But when he finally opened his eyes again, he saw that someone had covered him. And from the clock on the end table he knew that hours had passed.

He got up, stretched and walked over to the counter where he saw plates of food covered with plastic—one of sandwiches and one of pastries. They were next to a machine that apparently produced any kind of hot beverage you wanted.

He opted for black coffee, which he sipped while he ate half a roast beef sandwich and all of a cherry Danish—the first real food he'd had in a long time, he realized.

When he'd finished, he investigated the bathroom, where he found a set of clean clothes on a counter across from the shower.

Twenty minutes later, he was feeling a lot more human. And while he brushed his teeth and shaved, he wondered where he could find Lily. In fact, when he stepped back into the lounge, he saw that she was sitting on the couch opposite where he'd been sleeping.

She gave him a critical inspection. "How are you?"

"I'm fine, Dr. Wardman. What about you?"

"Kind of overwhelmed. A lot has happened in the past few days—and not what I expected."

"Yeah," he agreed. "I'm back from the dead."

"You weren't dead."

"Thanks to you,"

"I ..."

"Don't be modest. You saved me when I insisted on coming back here."

241

She answered with a little nod. He swept his hand toward the drink machine. "What can I get you?"

"A latte."

"Fancy."

"I deserve it."

"Yeah."

He brought her the drink and sat down opposite her.

There was so much he wanted to say—and ask, but he wasn't sure where to start.

"You look really serious," she said, "What were you thinking about?"

"Us."

The word hung in the air between them.

"And?"

Since he knew this was either going to be very good or very bad, he said, "I know we haven't known each other long. Not technically. But I want us to be together."

"I want that, too. Maybe I know you better than you know me. I could tell what kind of man you were when I read your background. Meeting you in the VR confirmed my opinion." She stopped and swallowed hard. "And I'm so sorry I had to go through that charade with you."

"Hamilton's rules."

"I should have questioned them."

"You did. But he was in charge."

They both stood, meeting in the middle of the room. Clasping her close, he allowed himself to feel happy for the first time in forever. As she raised her face, he lowered his mouth to hers for a kiss that went beyond basic need to outright greed. When he finally lifted his head a few inches, they were both out of breath.

His hands slid up and down her back, then cupped her bottom and pulled her against his erection.

"This is the first time we're going to be together in the real world," she whispered.

He looked around the lounge. "Are you saying you want to get a room in one of the hotels down the road?"

"Getting there would take at least twenty minutes. I don't think I can wait that long. In fact, I don't think I can make it across the room."

"Weak in the knees?"

"Too hot to walk."

"Lord, yes."

As they swayed together where they stood, he tugged her shirt over her head and tossed it away, then unhooked her bra and sent it following the shirt. When he was done, she dragged his knit shirt up and off.

His breath caught as he pulled her into his arms, absorbing the feel of her breasts against his naked chest while he stroked his hands along the silky skin of her back down to her narrow waist and over the curve of her hips. As he caressed her, he dragged her pants down. She kicked them away, and he stroked her naked bottom, entranced by the expanse of smooth softness.

She brought her hands up to cup his face, kissing him gently.

"I'm so thankful you're here," she murmured.

"Likewise."

"For a long time I focused on my work. Then I met a man who ... drew me, only he was out of reach."

He was overwhelmed by the deep emotion he heard in her voice. She gazed into his eyes as she ran her fingers over his face, down his neck, then bent to kiss his chest.

Raising her face to meet his gaze again, she unbuttoned his jeans and lowered the zipper enough to reach inside, taking his erection in her hand.

"You are so hot and hard for me."

"And all too ready." He looked back toward the couch, thinking it wasn't all that comfortable. Instead, he lifted her in his arms and carried her to the counter where he set her down near the edge and opened her legs. Standing between them, he kissed her breasts.

Catching her breath, she leaned back, bracing herself on her hands as he swirled his tongue around one distended nipple before sucking it into his mouth.

He took a step back, his chest tightening as he took in the passion on her face.

Then he bent and pulled her toward the edge of the counter, giving himself access to the most intimate part of her. He kissed her there, using his lips and tongue to caress her, loving the way her small sounds of pleasure told him how much she liked what he was doing.

"You're going to make me come," she gasped.

"That's the idea."

"Please. I want you in me."

He wanted that too, and he plunged into her, holding her on the counter as he stroked in and out of her, trying to wait for her as his need climbed.

Moments later, she cried out, and he followed her into the whirlwind. Afterwards, they clung together, both of them breathing hard.

He held her for satisfied moments before easing out of her. Picking her up, he carried her to the couch, where he lay back, covered them both, and cradled her in his arms.

She clasped him to her and rested her head on his shoulder.

"We're good together," she murmured.

"And we've got a head start on working out our relationship. Nothing like fighting monsters to find out what someone's made of."

"No more monsters."

"Except maybe in a video game."

They drifted comfortably in the afterglow of lovemaking. "I knew you were a good man before we ever spoke. And when I met you in the VR, I knew how right I was about you. It was so hard to think I'd never have you for real."

"And it made things worse for you not being able to tell me the truth."

"Yes," she whispered. He felt her swallow. "When you told me you were coming back here, I was so scared. I'd gotten to know you, and I was terrified you were going to end your life."

"It worked out okay."

"Thank God."

She stayed where she was for another few minutes, but he could tell she was thinking about easing away.

"What?"

She sat up and reached for the underwear she'd discarded.

"I've got to check on the patients and make sure everything's going okay. And Landon wants me to have a look at the new stuff he's working on. He's feeling a little shaky after his run-in with Preston."

"I'm sure." He stood and began finding his own clothing. "How long are you going to be?"

"A couple of hours."

"I'd like to meet the staff."

"Yes. Good idea. Frank knows some excellent specialists."

"Probably he kept up his contacts with the Naval Medical Center."

She nodded, and the look on her face told him she was thinking about something more.

"What?"

"Frank ..." She lifted one shoulder. "He seems to know a lot about virtual reality."

"From reading?"

"I don't think so. The way he talks, it makes me think he's been there."

"To Hamilton's VR?"

"Somewhere else."

"You could ask him."

"I think he'd avoid answering the question."

"Grant always said he hid his life outside work."

"I'd like to know about it. But I think I'll wait until he wants to say something.

Mack nodded, thinking he'd like to know, too. But he'd use Grant as his guide on all things Decorah.

Through the open bathroom door, he could see Lily finger combing her hair before she turned back to him.

"How do I look?"

"Beautiful."

She flushed. "I mean do I look like I've been making love?"

"Yeah."

Her flush deepened.

"Get used to it. You're going to be doing it a lot. And after you finish with the new staff and the patients, we can go find that hotel room."

EPILOGUE

Three weeks later.

Mack paused at the top of the broad staircase to the lobby level of the Mirador Hotel, thinking that Lily had made some good changes here—starting with having all the patients get together for an orientation meeting.

Well, all the adult patients. His eyes focused on Lily and the little girl who was sitting at a low table cutting out dresses for a paper doll.

When Shelly saw him standing on the upper level, she waved. Lily did the same, smiling as he joined them in the opulent space.

Shelly held up the dress she'd just cut out. "Should she wear this one, or should I do another?"

"Why don't you cut out another one, and we can see which looks best," he said, pleased that he was getting the hang of interacting with the little girl. "And while you do, I'm going to steal Lily away for a little while."

"Okay," Shelly agreed, returning to her paper and scissors.

When Lily got up, an attractive young woman glided over to the table. It was the robot nanny Lily had asked for to watch over Shelly when she couldn't be with her. The brunette, who looked like a woman in her early twenties, was

247

still a little wooden in her speech, but Landon was working on making her more realistic.

Shelly had named her Tinkerbell, straight out of her love for all things Disney.

Mack reached for Lily's hand and knitted his fingers with hers as they watched the girl and her nanny interacting for a few moments. Then they turned and walked down the covered walkway toward the bar.

"Shelly's adjusting nicely," Mack said. "And she likes Tink."

"Yes, the perfect companion. It was wonderful that I could move her over here." She paused, and he heard a catch in her voice. "But it's sad to think my sister's never going to grow up."

"Is perpetual childhood so bad? Didn't you love being a kid? And things got a lot more complicated when you grew up."

She thought for a moment. "Yes I did like my first decade. And the VR is certainly a million times better for Shelly than the existence she was living."

They rounded the corner and headed for the lawn where Paula Rendell was sitting at an easel painting a picture of a beautiful young woman dressed in a sari. She was one of the hotel staffers that Landon had also added to the VR to give the place a more authentic appeal. At this point they were still a little stilted, like Tinkerbell, but the designer was working on them, too.

"Nice," Mack said as studied the painting.

"I never had time to indulge my hobbies," Paula answered. She looked at Lily. "I'm grateful to be here."

"And we're glad to have you," Lily replied.

"And thanks for letting me talk to Landon."

"It gives him a better idea of what you need when he can hear it from you," Lily answered, then slid Mack a quick look. They, Grant and Frank Decorah had talked at length about the residents of the VR. Some, like Paula, Shelly and Ben

Todd were approved as permanent residents. Others, like Chris Morgan, were here, pending an investigation of their backgrounds. And Grant was still trying to get Jenny Seville to open up with him. They knew she had suffered some trauma, not just physically, but she was still afraid to say what it was.

Their outside investigations had led to a dead end. Apparently Jenny had turned up in the Union Memorial Emergency Room with no I.D. and no clue about her identity. The hospital staff had been happy to turn her over to Dr. Hamilton when he'd volunteered to take her off their hands. Had she hidden her identity? Or had someone else done it for her? Grant was still working on that.

After inspecting the swing set and play fort Landon had set up on the lawn, Mack and Lily headed back to the hotel. They were only spending a few hours in the VR this time because they both had a lot of work to do on the outside.

Mack and Grant were both working for Frank Decorah, not just as security for the VR. They were also taking some other jobs where they could use the telepathic powers that were growing stronger every day.

And Mack and Lily had found a nice apartment only ten minutes from the Decorah offices and the new Partners Lab, the name Lily had suggested for the facility.

Mack Bradley was still dead, as far as the world was concerned. And Frank Decorah had helped him work up a new identity, Maxwell Bailey, who had been born on Maryland's Eastern Shore and moved with his family around the mid-Atlantic area, so that he didn't have a long history in any one place.

Inside, they stopped to talk to Shelly, then headed upstairs to the room they now shared, where they could both use the gateway to the lab.

"See you in a little while," he said to Lily as he gave her a quick hug before watching her step inside what he still thought of as a "transporter."

He'd join her soon, in the new life he never could have imagined back in his Navy pilot days.

THE END

AFTERWORD

Thank you for purchasing Rx MISSING, I hope you enjoyed reading it as much as I loved writing it.

If you enjoy my books, do me a huge favor. Please go to your favorite online bookstore, and leave an honest review. Authors live and die by their reviews. The few extra seconds it takes are really appreciated. Thank you!

DECORAH SECURITY SERIES
(sexy paranormal romantic suspense)
BY REBECCA YORK

#1. ON EDGE (e-book novella and Decorah prequel).

#2. DARK MOON (e-book and trade paperback novel).

#3. CHAINED (e-book novella).

#4. AMBUSHED (e-book short story).

#5. DARK POWERS (e-book and trade paperback novel).

#6. HOT AND DANGEROUS (e-book short story).

#7. AT RISK (e-book and trade paperback novel).

#8. CHRISTMAS CAPTIVE (e-book novella).

#9. DESTINATION WEDDING (e-book novella).

#10. RX MISSING (e-book and trade paperback novel)

DECORAH SECURITY COLLECTION (e-book including *Ambushed, Hot and Dangerous, Chained,* and *Dark Powers*).

OFF-WORLD SERIES
(sexy science-fiction romance)
BY REBECCA YORK

#1. HERO'S WELCOME (e-book romance short story).

#2. NIGHTFALL (e-book romance novella).

#3. CONQUEST (e-book romance short story).

#4. ASSIGNMENT DANGER (e-book romance novella).

#5. CHRISTMAS HOME (e-book romance short story).

#6. FIRELIGHT CONFESSION (e-book romance novella)

OFF WORLD COLLECTION (e-book including *Nightfall, Hero's Welcome,* and *Conquest*).

PRAISE FOR REBECCA YORK

Rebecca York delivers page-turning suspense.
—Nora Roberts

Rebecca York never fails to deliver. Her strong characterizations, imaginative plots and sensuous love scenes have made fans of thousands of romance, romantic suspense and thriller readers.
—Chassie West

Rebecca York will thrill you with romance, kill you with danger and chill you with the supernatural.
—Patricia Rosemoor

(Rebecca York) is a real luminary of contemporary series romance
—Michael Dirda, The Washington Post Book World

Rebecca York's writing is fast-paced, suspenseful, and loaded with tension.
—Jayne Ann Krentz

ABOUT THE AUTHOR

A New York Times and USA Today Best-Selling Author, Rebecca York is a 2011 recipient of the Romance Writers of America Centennial Award. Her career has focused on romantic suspense, often with paranormal elements.

Her 16 Berkley books and novellas include her nine-book werewolf "Moon" series. KILLING MOON was a launch book for the Berkley Sensation imprint. She has written for Harlequin, Berkley, Dell, Tor, Carina Press, Silhouette, Kensington, Running Press, Tudor, Pageant Books, and Scholastic.

Her many awards include two Rita finalist books. She has two Career Achievement awards from Romantic Times: for Series Romantic Suspense and for Series Romantic Mystery. And her Peregrine Connection series won a Lifetime Achievement Award for Romantic Suspense Series.

Many of her novels have been nominated for or won RT Reviewers Choice awards. In addition, she has won a Prism Award, several New Jersey Romance Writers Golden Leaf awards and numerous other awards.

Web site: www.RebeccaYork.com
E-mail: rebecca@rebeccayork.com
Facebook: www.facebook.com/ruthglick
Twitter: @rebeccayork43
Blog: www.rebeccayork.blogspot.com

Made in the USA
Charleston, SC
03 November 2015